D0463376

The Puzzle in the Portrait

Eleanor Florence Rosellini

Illustrations by Elizabeth Vogt

GUILD PRESS OF INDIANA, INC.

GUILD PRESS OF INDIANA, INC.
435 Gradle Drive
Carmel, Indiana 46032
TELEPHONE: 317-848-6421
WWW. GUILDPRESS.COM

ISBN 1-57860-026-X

Library of Congress
Catalog Card Number
99-71651

Cover art by Elizabeth Vogt
Cover designed by Steven D. Armour
Text designed by Sheila G. Samson

Printed and bound in the United States of America

To Jay, Alissa, and Stefan
To friends who never let me quit
And to all the storytellers in my family

Keeper of memories,
Bearer of tales,
Spinning yesterday into golden threads,
Passed hand to hand
through time and generations.

A Puzzling Phone Call

July 12th. Williams Bay, Wisconsin. Just arrived at grand-father's house. Brother is running around birdbath, waving a stick and grunting like a cave man.

Elizabeth Pollack smiled as she closed her journal. Someday she would write a book about her brother. No doubt about it. Jonathan had to be shared with the world.

She slid out of the car and watched. Jonathan was definitely a challenge. He had just turned eight, and was restless and wiry. And nosy as a raccoon. Elizabeth put on her big-sister voice. "Would you quit snorting? You're scaring the chipmunks." Jonathan came to a stop and raised his stick in the air. His sandy brown hair stood on end, whipped up by a stiff summer breeze. "An ancient warrior dance!" he shouted. "From Outer Mongolia! It's supposed to bring an adventure." He added one last grunt.

Elizabeth shook her head slowly. "Jonathan? Why are you so weird?"

Jonathan trotted after her as she walked to the back door. "I'm not weird. You said you were tired of playing detective. And you want a real mystery. So I'm trying to get us one."

"Get us a mystery? Here?" Elizabeth turned away and rolled her eyes. Their grandfather's roomy wooden house was about as mysterious as an old slipper. No secret chambers or trap doors. Just a plain, grey two-story on a shady hill. Down below, a sunlit bay opened onto a long, deep lake, busy with boats. "Forget about grunting, Jonathan. There's no mystery here."

"Oh, I wouldn't be too sure about that." Their mother walked from the car, looking small behind the bulky black suitcase she carried. "There *is* something about this house," said Mrs. Pollack, "but . . . I haven't thought about it for a long time." She stopped by the back door. Her brown eyes squinted up toward the sky, as if she were trying to see something very far away. "You know the old portrait. The one that hangs in the living room. I used to think that was very mysterious."

"What do you mean?" Elizabeth had never paid much attention to the painting. She could vaguely remember a man with a long beard and unfriendly eyes.

"I know! It's the beard!" Jonathan began dancing around the birdbath again. "I bet the beard in the picture is growing. It's getting longer and longer. It's going to grow right out of the frame. It's going to start creeping across the room and wrapping around people's legs. And . . . and there's probably some kind of family curse. Right?"

Mrs. Pollack laughed. "Well, nothing quite like that. Just a family story. Let's see. According to the story, my great-grandmother Lydia talked about that painting just before she died. She kept saying it should never, *ever* be sold or given away. She made the whole family give a solemn promise. As if the painting was very important or had some kind of secret."

Elizabeth reached out as Mrs. Pollack opened the screen door. "Mom, wait! Didn't you ever look for the secret?"

"I did try once. Come to think of it, I must have been about eleven years old. Exactly your age, Elizabeth. I remember climbing up on a chair and looking over the whole painting with a magnifying glass. I didn't find any secret though. I don't think anybody else did either. Anyway, you can ask Pop about it."

"Ask Pop? Well, uh, maybe you should ask him."

Jonathan nodded. Pop was not a cozy, storybook kind of grand-father. He was grumpy and hard, like a table with sharp corners. Espe-cially since Gran died.

Elizabeth and Jonathan let their mother go in first. They fol-lowed her into a large, creaky kitchen, with a scuffed wooden floor and blue flowers fading on the wallpaper. Pop was nowhere to be seen.

Elizabeth stood in the middle of the room and closed her eyes. Her detective handbook said people use their eyes too much. A good detective had to feel and hear and smell, not just see. With her eyes still shut, Elizabeth concentrated on Pop's kitchen. Cigar smoke. A hint of bacon grease and hot dogs. And a wheezy hum from the old, round-shouldered refrigerator.

"Hey, Mom, guess what! Elizabeth is in a . . . in a . . . trance." Jonathan snapped his fingers in front of her face. "You will now wake up and start clucking like a chicken."

"Jonathan, leave me alone. I'm trying to practice my detective skills." Elizabeth lifted her head and gave the air an expert sniff. "Pop had bacon for breakfast, broiled hot dogs for lunch, smoked a cigar, and then . . ." She heard long, slow snores, trembling in the air like distant thunder. "And then he went into the den to take a nap."

Mrs. Pollack set down her suitcase. "Okay, Sherlock Holmes. Let's go see if you're right."

"Into the lion's den," whispered Jonathan. They tiptoed single file through the living room, weaving past sturdy armchairs and marble-topped tables. Elizabeth stayed behind the others. She wasn't thinking about mysteries and old portraits now. She was thinking about Pop. He was all right once she got used to him. But at first . . . She took a deep breath and caught up with Jonathan.

The den was a dim, narrow room, crammed with books and travel souvenirs. Pop sat dozing on a worn, red couch. His half-smoked cigar smoldered in an ashtray.

Elizabeth stayed in the doorway with Jonathan. Their grandfa-ther snored softly, his face half buried in a pillow. Elizabeth could see one sandpaper cheek, grey and wrinkled, like the bark of a very old tree. And just above him—something new. Pop's collection of wooden masks had come out of the trunk. They hung scowling on the wall now. Fierce-looking faces with empty eyes and open mouths.

"Dad, we're here." Mrs. Pollack placed a slender hand on her father's shoulder. Pop straightened up stiffly, smoothing back a few thin grey hairs. "Well?" His voice erupted in a low rumble. "What do you do when you see your grandfather?" After receiving brief pecks on the cheek, he squinted at Elizabeth. "What happened to your hair?"

Elizabeth straightened her glasses and tucked a loose strand of hair behind her ear. She could feel her long ponytail drooping like a wilted flower.

"Elizabeth looks just fine, Dad." Mrs. Pollack spoke a little sharply. "We've been in the car all day, and it's very hot outside."

Elizabeth glanced at Jonathan. *His* hair looked like the day after a tornado. "Where's your cat, Pop?" Jonathan dropped to the floor, out of Pop's view. He stuck his head underneath the couch. "And what's her name? I forgot."

"She doesn't have a name. I just call her *Cat*." Pop lifted himself off the couch. "Don't bother about the cat. She doesn't like children. Anyway, I want to give you two a test. To see how observant you are."

A test? During summer vacation? Elizabeth and Jonathan shuffled into the living room behind Pop. The wide picture window showed two sailboats skimming across the lake. The silky blue water looked warm. Perfect for swimming.

"Pay attention!" Pop banged three times on a long marble coffee table. "I want you to tell me what's missing. Right there." He pointed to the dark-paneled wall, just above a stiff black couch.

Elizabeth turned around and looked up. "Oh, no! The picture of the man with the beard is gone! Mom was just telling us about it."

"Not *picture*. It's a *painting*—a portrait of my great-grandfather, Joshua Bailey." Elizabeth and Jonathan exchanged glances.

"You didn't sell it, did you?" asked Jonathan. "You aren't supposed to."

"Of course I didn't sell it. The frame needed to be fixed. I sent the painting to a place in Walworth." Pop wagged a thin finger at Jonathan. "You have to take care of old family things. Keep them fixed up. Of course, no one cares about old things any more."

"Mom cares about old things," said Elizabeth. "She teaches history, and she—"

"Computers!" Pop spit the word out like poison. "That's all people care about. Or watching television. Idiot box! That's what I call it!" He was interrupted by the jangle of the telephone.

Pop answered with an irritated *Hello.* "I can't hear you! I'm eighty-one years old. You have to speak up." He paused, then thrust the telephone into Elizabeth's hands. "It's Mr. Lattimore. The man who's repairing the frame. See what he wants. I can't hear him."

"But, Pop, I . . . don't you think Mom should talk?" It was no use. Mrs. Pollack was outside unpacking the car. Jonathan edged away, suddenly interested in Pop's travel souvenirs. He picked up a long brass elephant prod from the coffee table.

When the conversation was over, Elizabeth still gripped the telephone receiver. "He said we can pick up the painting. As long as we get there before five o'clock." She looked up as her mother walked into the room. "But it's kind of strange. Mr. Lattimore said he found something . . . mysterious when he took off the frame."

"What did he find?" Jonathan struck a heroic pose with the elephant prod.

"He didn't say. He said he'd show us when we get there." Elizabeth stared at the empty spot on the wall. The secret of the old portrait. Mr. Lattimore must have found it.

Jonathan hung on his mother's arm. "We can pick it up today, can't we? And find out about the mystery?"

"Well, I have to call home and tell Dad we got here all right. And it's already after four o'clock. Besides, I've been driving all day."

Elizabeth gave Jonathan a nudge. They had to do something. Fast. Before their mother said *no.* "A nice rest. That's what you need. You just sit here, Mom." Elizabeth dragged a padded rocking chair next to the picture window. Jonathan handed Mrs. Pollack a glass of water and dropped a comic book into her lap. "We'll finish unpacking the car, Mom. Then we can leave."

"Oh, all right." Mrs. Pollack leaned back with a yawn. Pop pointed up the stairs. "Elizabeth in the quilt room. Jonathan in the bedroom across the hall."

A few minutes later Elizabeth bounced her backpack onto a narrow bed topped with a worn patchwork quilt. The tiny room was her favorite spot—windows on three sides and the best view of the lake. It felt as high and breezy as a crow's nest.

Jonathan appeared in the doorway. "You can come in, Jonathan. But no grunting." Suddenly Pop's voice boomed up the stairs. "Shut the bedroom door! Do *not* let Cat into the room!"

Elizabeth pulled Jonathan into the room and whipped the door shut. She wrinkled her nose. Pop's cranky black cat had some bad habits. Like using the bedrooms as a litter box.

"We'll let Mom rest ten more minutes." Elizabeth knelt in front of a small bookcase and pulled a mystery story from the bottom shelf. Jonathan stared at the torn paper cover. A man in a black cape shined his flashlight on a ragged piece of map.

Jonathan grabbed the book. "A treasure map! That man who cleaned Pop's painting. He could have found some kind of treasure map."

"I don't think so." Elizabeth grabbed the book back. "But there could be another painting. In this one mystery I read, there were two paintings in one frame. And the one hidden underneath was really old. And worth a lot of money."

A few minutes later, Elizabeth checked her watch. Twenty minutes to five. They could make it if they left now. She stuck her head out the bedroom door.

"Mom! It's time to go." Elizabeth felt something soft as she opened the door, like a feather brushing her ankle. She looked down to see the tip of a fat black tail disappear under her bed. "Oh, great! The cat."

Jonathan lifted the quilt and uncovered a pair of unblinking green eyes. Elizabeth peered at a stack of folding chairs stored under the bed. "Okay, Jon. Just don't scare her. If she gets behind those chairs, we'll never get her out. And if she makes a mess in there, we're really in trouble."

Pop's slow, heavy footstep sounded on the wooden stairs. "What are you doing up there? We've got to go. Right now."

"Uh . . . we're coming. You don't have to come up here—really!" Jonathan bent down. "Nice kitty. Come to Jonathan. I have a present for you." The cat narrowed her eyes and backed up farther under the bed.

Elizabeth wiped her forehead with the back of her hand. Seventeen minutes to five. "Emergency plan number one." Turning her head to the side, she dangled her long ponytail in front of the bed. Success. Jonathan untangled the chubby black cat from Elizabeth's hair.

He raced down the stairs and plopped the cat in the middle of Pop's old red couch. Elizabeth glanced out the window at the top of the stairs. "Come on. We get to ride in the big car!" They rushed outside and scrambled into the back of Pop's old blue Chevy. Mrs. Pollack helped Pop into the passenger seat. Elizabeth let out a long breath as she leaned back on the wide seat. On to the mystery.

They left the lake behind and headed into the sunny Wisconsin countryside. Elizabeth ignored the tidy farmhouses and sleepy-looking cows. She imagined a stormy sky and dark castles on the horizon. And herself, of course. The world's most famous eleven-year-old detective. She closed her eyes, letting Mr. Lattimore's words slide into her mind. *I found something when I took off the frame. Something . . . mysterious.*

A Message from the Past

"Hey, asparagus-legs! Don't go to sleep!" Jonathan leaned over and shook his sister's arm.

Elizabeth narrowed her eyes. She *was* going to let Jonathan be her loyal assistant. But now—forget it. "Asparagus-legs? Where did you get that?"

"From your journal. I read it last night. You said you were too skinny and your legs look like stalks of asparagus." Jonathan ignored the gathering storm. "But you like your hair, because it's chocolate brown like Mom's. And you want to write a book about me. About how annoying I am. Like when I put the whoopee cushion under your pillow."

"Jonathan?" Elizabeth's voice became dangerously sweet. "Do you know what I'm going to do if you read my journal again?" She paused dramatically. "I'm going to pick out a girl in your class. I'm going to call her up. And I'm going to tell her that you love her." Jonathan made a gagging sound as he lunged across the back seat.

"All right, stop it! Both of you." Mrs. Pollack frowned into the rearview mirror. "We'll be picking up the painting in a minute." She pulled onto a small street near the center of Walworth. A few narrow storefronts crowded up against the sidewalk. Elizabeth leaned forward. She could see neat black letters painted on a dusty display window. EDWARD LATTIMORE. FURNITURE REPAIR. Her anger popped like a bubble and disappeared. They were about to find out about their mystery.

"Hello! Is anybody here?" Pop leaned over a long wooden counter at the front of the shop. A heavy brown curtain covered the doorway to the back room. Jonathan skipped up to the counter. "Ask him. Ask him what he found."

Pop waved him away. "Quiet down. First we get the painting."

A moment later the curtain parted, and a large, red-faced man filled the doorway. He wiped his hands on a stained white work apron. "Glad to see you, Mr. Emerson! I think you'll be pleased with the frame. Looks as good as new."

Mr. Lattimore held the curtain and motioned the others to follow. The back room was a clutter of furniture—tables, chairs, and dressers, half taken apart and half put together. In the corner, a round fan swiveled from side to side, pushing around the hot air. Elizabeth spotted the painting leaning against the skeleton of an old couch.

She watched as Mr. Lattimore lifted a white sheet covering the frame. The painting was even gloomier than she remembered. Pop's great-grandfather looked serious and grim, as if he had just given someone a good scolding. He had a long, bony nose and a fierce grey beard that plunged down to his chest.

"I'm glad people don't look like that any more." Jonathan backed up a step. Elizabeth glanced at her mother's wispy dark hair and soft features. Her mother was slim, like Pop. But her face didn't look a bit like his side of the family. Thank goodness.

Mr. Lattimore helped Mrs. Pollack carry the painting to the trunk of the car. Elizabeth leaned over and tucked the sheet over the portrait. When she straightened up, Pop was sitting in the car. Mr. Lattimore was gone.

"But what about the mystery?" As Elizabeth stepped toward the shop door, Mr. Lattimore rushed out, waving his hand.

"Wait a minute! I almost forgot to give you this." He walked over to Pop's open car window and handed him a small, yellowed piece of paper. "I found this when I took off the canvas. It was folded up, hidden behind the frame. Looks like some kind of . . . secret message." Mr. Lattimore frowned slightly. "But the writing is awfully faint. You probably won't be able to read it." Strange. He sounded almost relieved, as if he didn't want them to read it.

"And then I . . ." Mr. Lattimore never finished his sentence. Pop was already putting up the window and waving good-bye. Mr. Lattimore hesitated for a moment, then waved back as he returned to his shop.

"A secret message!" said Mrs. Pollack. "Just what you've been waiting for."

Elizabeth and Jonathan scrambled into the car, begging to see the note. Pop set it on the dashboard. "No one sees this until we get home. It's about to fall apart. You'll just end up ruining it."

The next hour was a blur of errands. Grocery store. Drugstore. In and out of the car. Elizabeth and Jonathan didn't even get a glimpse of the note. Pop's eagle eyes made sure of that.

"Last stop. Pop needs to pick up his mail." Mrs. Pollack pulled up to the post office and helped Pop out of the car. He soon returned with a handful of letters.

"All junk. And what's wrong with this blasted seat belt, anyway?" He made two fierce jabs before the buckle clicked into place.

Five more minutes and they were back at Pop's house. Elizabeth helped Pop out of the car. "Now we can look at—"

"You two get over there and hold the door open." Pop waved his arms and called to a young man sitting in the next yard. "We need some help here!"

The man shaded his eyes and squinted in their direction. "Sure, Mr. Emerson. Be right there."

Mrs. Pollack and Pop's neighbor carried the bulky portrait into the house. Pop shuffled after them with his hands fluttering. "Slow down! Careful of that frame, I tell you!"

"Pop, where's the secret message?" Jonathan tugged on the back of Pop's sleeve.

"It's still in the car. Now, don't bother us. We're busy."

Elizabeth and Jonathan rushed back to the car and flung open the door. Empty. The dashboard was empty.

Jonathan edged ahead as they ran back into the house. "Mom, the note! It's gone!" Mrs. Pollack and Pop's neighbor were standing on the old black couch, struggling to hang the painting.

"Sorry. Haven't seen it." Mrs. Pollack's arm shook under the weight of the painting.

Elizabeth turned to Pop. "You must have brought the paper in the house, Pop. It's not in the car."

"Well, if it's not in the car, I don't know where it is. I didn't bring it in."

Jonathan and Elizabeth started over. They groped around in all the gritty corners of the car. They rushed through the kitchen, turning over every piece of paper in sight. But the secret message had vanished. And so had their mystery.

Jonathan sank down on a high-backed kitchen chair. Elizabeth paced across the floor, then stopped and snapped her fingers. "We need expert advice! And I know where to find it." She pulled out a thick leather book from her backpack. The title was stamped in gold letters on the cover. *How to Think Like a Detective.* As soon as he spotted the book, Jonathan leaped out of his chair and headed in the opposite direction.

"Not so fast." Elizabeth chased him around the long kitchen table. Finally, she grabbed his arm. "There's a whole chapter about finding things."

"No! Don't start reading that dumb book to me again! You think you're some kind of professor. Just because Mom and Dad are teachers." Jonathan squirmed but Elizabeth held tight.

"I'm not going to read the whole thing. Just listen to this: *Most people spend too much time looking and not enough time thinking. Try this method. First, think about when you last saw the missing item. Next, picture in your mind exactly what you did from that time on.*"

Jonathan quit squirming. "Okay, you can let go. I remember something. When Pop was in the post office with Mom, I got in the front seat. The note was still on the dashboard. But I saw Pop coming, so I didn't touch it."

Elizabeth closed her eyes and imagined herself back in the car. "Pop was holding the mail, then he got in the car. He had trouble putting on his seat belt." Elizabeth began pacing again. "I bet he put the letters up on the dashboard when he was trying to get his belt on. And when he picked up the letters, he must have picked up the piece of paper too."

"Then I know just where to look!" Jonathan ran across the room and stuck his arm into a paper bag next to the wastebasket. He pulled out three unopened envelopes, a garden catalog, and . . . the old note. "Elementary, my dear Watson. Our mystery was going to get recycled with Pop's junk mail."

Elizabeth stood by the kitchen table as Jonathan unfolded the paper. He smoothed it out on the pale blue tablecloth. The note was yellow and brittle, not much bigger than a postcard. Elizabeth let out a groan as she peered at the faint brown writing. Mr. Lattimore was right. She couldn't read a word.

"I know what we need!" Jonathan rushed through the kitchen, opening and closing drawers. Finally, he held up a small, round magnifying glass. "Just like a real detective."

Elizabeth heard Mrs. Pollack at the front door saying good-bye to Pop's neighbor. "Mom, come in here! We found the paper."

"It was with Pop's junk mail," said Jonathan. "And we figured it out just by thinking. Like Sherlock Holmes."

As Mrs. Pollack watched, Jonathan held the magnifying glass above the paper. "I see numbers!" He leaned over, closer to the note. "At the top. One. Eight. And then . . . seven. And nine."

Elizabeth grabbed a pencil and a pad of note paper from the kitchen counter. She wrote down the numbers. "One-eight-seven-nine. Jonathan! That's 1879. Over a hundred years ago."

The three of them bent over the note, straining to make out the words. After a few minutes, they had deciphered a few parts of the message. Elizabeth wrote down the letters.

1879

L. E.
Now __ __ __m_ __ __ ___ ___ ___ l___. Where __
l___ _____ __fear ___ __. ____ ___ m_____
_____ _____r t___ the ____. _____
__— __o__ __a__ it _____ __a__ ___ not.

A _____

Jonathan ran into the den. "Pop, guess what!"

Pop sat on the red couch underneath his wooden masks. He fanned himself with a magazine. "Go to the window and look at the lake. You'll never see anything prettier."

Jonathan shot a glance at the pink and gold sunset. "Right. Really nice. But, Pop. That old piece of paper is a note! We can't figure out many of the words. But it's really old—1879."

Elizabeth bounced onto the couch next to Pop. "It was written to someone with the initials *L. E.*, and it . . . Wait. What did you say your grandmother's name was?"

"Lydia. Lydia Bailey. After she got married, her name was Lydia Emerson."

"*L. E.*," said Mrs. Pollack slowly. "Lydia Emerson. Maybe the note was written to your grandmother."

Pop pointed to a bulky desk in the corner. "There's a red folder in the top drawer. *Emerson Family Genealogy.* You go get it, Jonathan."

"Aye-aye, cap'n!" Jonathan gave a crisp salute. Pop answered with a not-so-angry snort. "And where are my blasted glasses?" Pop ran his hands along the couch, then pulled a crooked pair of reading glasses from behind the cushion. Elizabeth and Jonathan peered over his shoulder, as he opened the red folder. Nothing but names and dates. Pop slowly turned the typewritten pages. "Just as I thought. My grandmother is the only one with the initials *L. E.* The note was definitely written to her."

Elizabeth scribbled down the information before Pop closed the folder. *Lydia Bailey. Born 1854. Married William Emerson in 1875. Died in 1941.*

Jonathan shook his head. "But how did the note get hidden in the picture frame? And anyway, who's the guy in the painting? I forgot."

"Not *guy!*" Pop's mouth drooped into a scowl. "*Man.* Who's the *man* in the painting!"

Mrs. Pollack turned to Jonathan. "The *man* in the painting is Grandma Lydia's father, Joshua Bailey. After he died, Grandma Lydia inherited the painting. She had it for years."

Elizabeth rose slowly from the couch. "And that's why she made everyone promise to keep the painting. She knew the note was hidden there. And she knew someone would find it after she died." Elizabeth gazed out the window at the dark, smooth water of the lake. It was the glowing time of day—just before dark—when the world looks soft and still. And mysterious.

Pop struggled up off the couch. "Let me take a look at that paper." He followed the others to the kitchen table and picked up the note. "I've never seen this before. But . . ." He handed the note to Elizabeth. "Show me exactly how this was folded up."

Elizabeth laid the paper on the blue tablecloth. She folded the right side toward the middle and did the same with the left. "It was like this, Pop. The ends were folded over so they meet in the middle." She looked up. "Does that mean something?"

"It certainly does. My grandmother had an unusual way of folding things. Most people just fold things in half. She always folded paper just like this. Both ends toward the middle." Pop lowered himself into a chair. "My grandmother saw this note, and she was the one who hid it."

Mrs. Pollack put her hand on Pop's shoulder. "So someone wrote a note to Grandma Lydia in 1879. But why did she hide it? And why is the word *fear* in the message? What was there to be afraid of?"

For a moment no one spoke. This was no make-believe mystery. The faded letters carried a message from the past, a secret message hidden in a portrait for over one hundred years.

Elizabeth slid the note gently into her hand. A family mystery. And it had been there all the time, waiting and waiting to be discovered.

The Investigation Begins

> ELIZABETH AND JONATHAN POLLACK
> ACE DETECTIVES FOR HIRE

Elizabeth taped the small, hand-lettered sign to the door of the quilt room. "Come on, Jon. We need to get started."

She tied a sweatshirt around her shoulders, then sat down on a soft grey rug next to her bed. Dinner was over, and the lake whispered through the window on a cool night breeze. Elizabeth set her detective handbook on the floor in front of her. "The first meeting of the Pollack Detective Agency will now come to order."

Jonathan crawled into the room, bent over Pop's magnifying glass. He studied a large black ant marching across the floorboards. "Hey, Elizabeth! Ants can milk aphids, you know. Just like people milk cows. Wanna know how?" Jonathan didn't wait for an answer. "See, aphids are these little green bugs that suck plant juice. And then they digest it, and it comes out the other end. And the ants sort of . . ."

"Jonathan! The mystery. Remember?"

Jonathan put down the magnifying glass. "But I don't get it. What are we supposed to do?"

"We just . . . Well, we . . ." Elizabeth glanced at a moth fluttering against the screen. "We have to get *organized*. Like my detective handbook says. First we need a casebook. Something we can carry with us to write everything down." She rummaged through her backpack and pulled out a spiral notebook with a shiny red cover. *The Puzzle in the Portrait*. Elizabeth printed the letters across the first page with a bold purple marker. The next two pages were marked *Evidence* and *Background*.

"Tomorrow we'll look at the note again. And when we figure out more words, we'll put them on the page marked *Evidence*. Then we need to ask Pop about his grandmother Lydia." Elizabeth closed the notebook and stuck her favorite green pen into the spiral binding. "Sort of like interviewing a witness."

Jonathan stood up. "I don't think Pop wants to answer a lot of questions. It seems like he's mad all the time. And he probably doesn't even like us."

"Well, Mom says he does. I don't know. Maybe being crabby is just a habit. Like when people can't stop biting their fingernails. Anyway, I think we should . . ." She reached into her backpack and pulled out a small white bag. "I think we should give Pop a test tomorrow. See if he likes having us around."

Jonathan sat back down with a smile. He glanced at the door and made sure it was shut.

The next morning, Elizabeth and Jonathan followed the smell of bacon to the kitchen. Pop, wrapped in an old yellow apron that Gran used to wear, stood grumbling in front of the stove.

Jonathan looked around the room. "Hi, Pop. Where's Mom?"

"*Hi?* What do you mean, *Hi?*" Pop poked a fork in Jonathan's direction. "When you first see someone you say *Good morning.*" Elizabeth sighed. She wished Pop would stop trying to improve people all the time. Pop tossed a handful of silverware onto the table. "Your mother's in the back room looking for the syrup pitcher. You two set the table."

A few minutes later Pop shuffled to the table with a plate of steaming pancakes. Suddenly the plate tilted. He drew back and grabbed Elizabeth by the shoulder.

"Get a shoe! Get a shoe and swat the blasted thing!"

"What are you talking about, Pop?"

"That!" Pop pointed to the table. A dark brown cockroach, as big as a thumb, sat on the tablecloth next to his plate. Mrs. Pollack hurried into the kitchen. Pop stood next to the table waving his hands. Elizabeth and Jonathan pressed themselves against the wall, shrieking. Then Elizabeth stopped screaming. Calmly, she reached over and picked up the bug.

"Don't worry, Pop, it's just fake. It's kind of a . . . test." Elizabeth held the plastic bug in front of Pop's face. He threw up his hands and entertained them with a few loud screams. He sat down with a chuckle and didn't even complain about the cold pancakes.

Elizabeth nodded at Jonathan. At least they didn't have to worry about Pop not liking them. He had passed the test with an *A*.

After breakfast, Elizabeth picked up the red detective notebook and motioned to Jonathan. Time to interview Pop. They found him in a wide, high-backed chair, gazing out the living room window. He leaned back with his cigar, puffing lazy clouds of smoke like a contented dragon. Let's hope he doesn't start breathing fire, thought Elizabeth. She sat next to Jonathan on the black couch. The leather seat felt hard, more like a church pew than a sofa. "Pop, we want to—"

"What? I can't hear you." Pop cupped his hand behind his ear. "Don't be afraid of the sound of your own voice! Speak up and speak well!"

Elizabeth straightened up and flipped open her notebook. "We want to find out more about your grandmother."

"So you're interested in my grandmother, are you?" Pop cleared his throat and slapped a cigar ash off his knee. "Well, to understand Grandma Lydia, you have to understand how she grew up. The Baileys were wealthy, you see—owned a lot of farmland. Prairie land, some of the best in Ohio. Grandma Lydia had the finest of everything. But it wasn't always like that." Pop suddenly leaned toward Jonathan. "How would you like to be sent away from home and go work on a farm, Sonny-boy?" Pop's voice was sharp as a knife, as if Jonathan should start packing his bags right away.

"Uh, well, I . . ."

"That's what happened to Grandma Lydia's father, Joshua Bailey." Pop pointed to the thin, stern face in the portrait. "It was back in 1816. The family had just come to Ohio and put all their savings in the local bank. Next thing you know the bank closes and never gives their money back. Eight children and no money. So Joshua Bailey was sent away to work on a farm. And he was only ten years old! Ten!" Pop waved his cigar at Jonathan. "Later Joshua Bailey went west and earned money as a cattle driver. Little by little he saved enough to come back to Ohio and start buying farmland. You think that face in the portrait looks mean, don't you? Well, those lines in his face are from a life of hard work. Just plain hard work."

1816. Bank lost money. Age ten. Farm hand. Later cattle driver. Elizabeth's hand flew across the page. Jonathan swatted at a cloud of cigar smoke.

"So there were two things Grandma Lydia learned from her father. Now, write this down in your notebook. First, she never turned away anyone in need. And second, she never put her money in a bank. Not a penny."

Elizabeth wiggled her stiff fingers. She was learning something about Grandma Lydia, but not much about the mystery. "But what about the note, Pop? Did Grandma Lydia ever say anything about it?"

"The note? No, she never mentioned the note. But . . . she did say something strange just before she died. My father told me about it." Pop took a thoughtful puff on his cigar. "She was talking about the portrait, making everyone promise never to sell it. Then she tried to tell my father something. She was so weak, he could barely hear her. He understood only two words . . . *the thirteenth.* That was all. No one knew what she meant."

"*The thirteenth?*" Elizabeth wrote the words in her notebook. It wasn't much of a clue. "You mean, a date? Like the thirteenth of June or something?"

Pop shrugged. "My father didn't think she was talking about a date. Of course, no one really knows."

"But . . ." Jonathan slid down from the couch and stood next to Pop's chair. "There has to be something else, Pop. Wasn't there anything mysterious about your grandmother?"

"Well, her parlor was gloomy. She always kept it dark, with the shades down and sheets over the chairs. But lots of people did that to protect the furniture. No, Grandma Lydia was a good, kindhearted woman. And smart too. She was a school teacher before she was married. No, not mysterious, except . . . well, except her clock."

Pop turned in his chair and pointed to the wide stone fireplace. On the mantel above stood a delicate wooden clock, rounded at the top, like an arch. The thin metal hands on the front were frozen at five minutes after two. "That clock used to be in the parlor. Right underneath the portrait of Joshua Bailey. Grandma Lydia called it her fortune-teller clock."

Pop stood up and opened a small glass door at the front of the clock. He gave the brass pendulum a gentle push. It swung for a moment, then hung still.

"You see, this old clock has a mind of its own. Sometimes it doesn't run for years. Just like now. Then, one day, you start the pendulum, and the clock starts ticking again. My grandmother took that as a sign." Pop spoke through a swirl of cigar smoke. "A sign that something was about to happen. Something good or something bad."

Elizabeth gazed at the clock, sitting silent and still. She didn't know why, but Pop's house was beginning to feel different. Like a storybook, full of tales about the past. "Did any more of your furniture belong to Grandma Lydia? I mean, we might find something hidden. More clues."

Pop thought for a moment. "The wooden blanket chest in the den. And the high dresser in the quilt room. Those belonged to my grandparents." He pointed to the black leather couch. "And that couch you're sitting on. My grandfather made it himself." Jonathan dove down and began poking his fingers into the corners of the sofa. Pop rushed over. "Careful now! Don't break anything!"

Elizabeth stood at the bottom of the stairway a few minutes later.

They had found nothing in the couch, except the cat's hiding place underneath. Jonathan earned an angry scratch for that. The blanket chest had no clues either, just an old hairpin and a smelly piece of mothball stuck in a crack. Elizabeth picked up her detective notebook. The dresser in the quilt room. Maybe that hid a secret.

Again, Pop's voice followed them up the stairs. "Shut the bedroom door! Do *not* let Cat into the room!"

Jonathan and Elizabeth scurried into the room. The dark old dresser was squeezed into a corner behind the door. They pulled out four wide drawers and set them on the floor. They searched among the socks and thick wool sweaters. Nothing interesting. Finally, Elizabeth shined her flashlight into the shell of the dresser. There, where the top drawer had been. Her beam of light caught a glint of metal. Something was stuck between two pieces of wood. She reached in and pulled out a tiny metal key.

"We found something behind the drawer!" They burst into the den and startled Pop out of a doze. Their mother came in from the living room.

Pop sat up and squinted at the flat, shiny key. "This looks familiar. It must have fallen behind the drawer. But I have no idea what it opens."

"Something small," said Mrs. Pollack. "A suitcase, maybe." Elizabeth and Jonathan tried every keyhole in the house. The key fit none of them.

"I give up." Elizabeth dropped the key into the top dresser drawer. She sat on her bed with her red casebook. They didn't have much to go on. A note they couldn't read. The words *the thirteenth*, mumbled just before Grandma Lydia died. And now a tiny key that fit no lock. Elizabeth leaned back against the wall. The note. They *had* to figure out the note. And they only had two more days.

But the weather was sunny and the lake was warm, and Pop's old brown rowboat waited at the pier. Sometimes they forgot the mystery, but never for long. They always came back, sitting at the long kitchen table, hunched over the note. Mrs. Pollack even dug out some old family letters so they could practice reading old-fashioned handwriting.

"That's it, Jon. I feel like we've looked at this note a million times." Elizabeth took off her glasses and rubbed her eyes. "We're just not going to figure out any more letters. And tomorrow we have to leave."

Elizabeth picked up the note. The secret of the old portrait was here. Right at her fingertips. They had deciphered more words, but not enough to understand the message. It was like finding a chest full of gold and not having the key.

She pushed the notebook across the table to Jonathan. "This is all we have."

> *1879*
>
> *L. E.*
> *Now i_ __ __m_ to _____ __at _____ lost. Where __ l___*
> *_____en I fear __ __y. But t___ m_____g t___ps*
> *___e___r tell the tale. _____em_r*
> *t__ — __o__ have it _____ have it not.*
>
> *A _____d*

Elizabeth stood on tiptoe and slipped the old note on the mantel next to Grandma Lydia's clock. "I guess we can forget about being world-famous."

When it was time to leave the next morning, Elizabeth and Jonathan filed down the stairs with their suitcases. Jonathan's steps slowed. Pop was standing in the living room, staring at them with his arms crossed.

"You two come over here. I want to give you something." Pop uncrossed his arms. He was holding the old note. "No use leaving it here. You two are the detectives in the family." He handed the yellowed piece of paper to Elizabeth.

"And don't ruin it." Pop marched out of the room before they could thank him.

"Jonathan! I can't believe Pop gave us the note. I didn't—" Elizabeth stopped. A unfamiliar sound startled her, like a sudden tap on the shoulder. She whirled around. The clock. Grandma Lydia's fortune-teller clock. It was ticking.

Mr. Lattimore Has More to Tell

Jonathan shot out the back door in front of Elizabeth. He leaped up and landed in front of Pop. "Guess what! Grandma Lydia's clock is ticking! And I bet it's because of our mystery." But the adults only half listened. Pop scowled as Mrs. Pollack squeezed the last suitcase into the trunk. "Why do you bring all that junk along? Travel light. That's what I say." He gave Elizabeth and Jonathan brief hugs, then herded them into the car. Elizabeth rolled down her window. "We'll let you know if we figure out any—"

"Slow down!" shouted Pop. He waved his hands in the air as the car backed down the steep driveway. "Don't hit the rock! Watch that garbage can!"

Elizabeth slumped back against the seat. "Mom, how come Pop always interrupts people?"

"Well, he won't admit it, but his hearing isn't too good any more. He probably didn't even hear you." Mrs. Pollack tooted the horn as they drove away.

"Just like with Mr. Lattimore," said Jonathan. "He was right in the middle of a sentence. Pop just waved good-bye and rolled up his window."

Elizabeth stared at Jonathan. "Idiot!"

"Am not!"

"Not *you. Me*! I can't believe I forgot about that. Mr. Lattimore was trying to tell us something when Pop rolled up the window. It might be about the case." Elizabeth scooped up her red detective notebook. "We have to stop in Walworth and ask him."

Mrs. Pollack looked at her watch. "I don't know. It takes hours to get back to Indiana. Dad is expecting us for dinner, and we're already running late."

"But, Mom, we have to talk to him! We might be missing a big clue."

"Well . . . all right. But you have to make it quick. I'll pick you up after I go to the gas station."

A few minutes later Jonathan and Elizabeth stood on a crumbling sidewalk in front of Mr. Lattimore's shop. Their mother's small red car disappeared around the corner. Elizabeth marched up to the shop door, then hesitated. They didn't really know Mr. Lattimore. What if he didn't like kids? What if he didn't want to answer any questions? Clutching her detective notebook, she peeked through the shop window. No sign of Mr. Lattimore. Just the long counter and two empty wooden chairs.

Jonathan planted himself next to a parking meter. "You go talk to Mr. Lattimore. I'll stay here and watch for Mom." He backed up as Elizabeth walked toward him. "I'm not going in there. I don't know what to ask. And besides, his eyebrows look like . . . like big black caterpillars."

"Forget it. You're coming with me." Elizabeth dragged him through the door. The warm, heavy air smelled sharply of turpentine. "Mr. Lattimore must be working in the back room. Come on, Jon. He's not going to bite us. We just . . . aaugh!" Elizabeth's scream slipped out before she could stop it. Mr. Lattimore wasn't in back. He had been bending down, looking for something behind the counter. Now he popped up like a jack-in-the box and stood looming over

them. His great woolly eyebrows gave a slight twitch, as if they might get up and start crawling away.

"Well hello there! What can I do for you?" His voice was even louder than Pop's.

Jonathan couldn't take his eyes off Mr. Lattimore's forehead. "Uh . . . well . . . we want to ask you a few questions about that eyebrow." Elizabeth stared, wide-eyed, at her brother. "I mean, the note!" said Jonathan. "We wanted to ask you some questions about that note you found."

Mr. Lattimore chuckled. "Fire away! I'm all yours."

Elizabeth stepped in front of Jonathan. "We looked at the note you found. It's hard to read, but we figured out some of the words. It was written to our . . . let's see . . . our great-great-grandmother Lydia in 1879. The man in the painting is her father."

Mr. Lattimore stepped out from behind the counter. He sat down heavily on a creaky wooden chair. "Before you start, I need to tell you something. I tried to say this a few days ago, but your grandfather . . . well, your grandfather seemed to be in a hurry." Mr. Lattimore pulled out a checkered handkerchief and dabbed a bead of sweat from his forehead.

"Is it something about the note?" asked Jonathan. "Something mysterious?"

"Possibly." Mr. Lattimore paused. "You see, on the back of the frame, right next to the spot where the note was hidden, I saw some writing. I could make out the words *the thirteenth*." Elizabeth jumped as if pricked by a pin. Those were the words Grandma Lydia said just before she died.

"Just *the thirteenth*? Was there anything else?"

"There may have been a third word, but the wood was chipped and I couldn't see it. And that's not all. I saw three more words just below it. Strange words." Jonathan and Elizabeth stood on either side of Mr. Lattimore. They hardly dared to breathe. "*P. R. did it.*" Mr. Lattimore's deep voice made the words sound heavy and serious. "That's exactly what it said. *P. R. did it.*"

Elizabeth fumbled with her pen as she wrote the words in her notebook.

Mr. Lattimore frowned. "When I saw those words, I couldn't help but think—"

"That there was some kind of crime," said Elizabeth, "and the person who did it had the initials *P. R.*" She took a deep breath. The stuffy room seemed to be all heat and no air.

"Exactly. I think we've stumbled onto the traces of a crime committed a long time ago." Mr. Lattimore leaned back and set his rough hands on his knees. "Are you sure you want to try and read that note? I don't know. Maybe some secrets are better left alone."

"No way," said Jonathan. "We have to figure it out."

Elizabeth closed her notebook. "Jonathan and I want to be detectives. Real detectives. So we can't give up now. Besides, it couldn't be anything too terrible. If it was, Grandma Lydia would have torn up the note and burned it or something."

Mr. Lattimore stood up. "You know, you're right. You're both right. No self-respecting detectives would turn their backs on a good case like this!"

When Mrs. Pollack pulled up to the shop, Jonathan was jumping up and down on the sidewalk. "Another clue, Mom! A great one!" As they headed south toward home, Elizabeth stared at the *Evidence* page in her notebook. *The thirteenth. P. R. did it.*

But what did P. R. do? Some kind of crime? She barely lifted her head when her mother turned up the radio. Severe thunderstorm watch. Central Indiana.

Four hours later, it seemed the flat green fields would never end. Finally, the road dipped, then rose into a gentle hill. Elizabeth spotted the wide, brown Wabash River and a low bridge in the distance. Home was just over the next hill. A low growl of thunder made her wish they were already there.

"Mom, something weird is happening." Elizabeth peered out the car window. It was getting dark, too dark for a summer afternoon. At the edge of town, the streetlights flickered on. The last bit of daylight dimmed, then disappeared. Trees and houses were swallowed by a darkness black as midnight. "Don't worry. We're almost home." Mrs. Pollack's voice sounded high and tense.

Suddenly, a crash of thunder tore open the sky. The rain beat against the car, like an angry giant pounding to get in.

Elizabeth felt a flutter of fear. Her life used to be so . . . ordinary. But something changed, ever since the old note was found. The fortune-teller clock was ticking again. The words on the picture frame hinted of a crime. And now this storm. Changing day into night.

As Elizabeth squinted into the downpour, a flash of lightning gave a split-second view of home. Their boxy brick house never looked so safe and solid.

A tall, thin figure ran down the driveway under a black umbrella. Elizabeth stood on tiptoe and gave her father a wet hug.

"What a storm!" Mr. Pollack stood with the family on the back porch. His hazel eyes were bright, and his hair had taken on a wild look, just like Jonathan's. "And that cumulonimbus cloud! I've never seen a storm cloud block out the sunlight so completely. Extraordinarily dense." Mr. Pollack looked at the nervous faces of the rest of the family. "Of course, I'm sure you didn't enjoy it quite as much."

Elizabeth gave a shaky laugh. "I guess science teachers see things a little—"

A clap of thunder cut off the end of her sentence. The lights flickered, then went out. Tornado weather. Into the basement. No one had to say it.

Elizabeth didn't mind the musty coolness. The rough basement floor was solid as a rock. The wind and rain sounded muffled and far away. They gathered up some broken-down garden chairs and sat around a wobbly table. Mr. Pollack turned on a small radio.

A tiny voice came out of the darkness. "Hands up, dumbo! You're under arrest!"

Elizabeth lit a candle. "It's not the radio, Dad. It's just Fritzi. We couldn't leave him upstairs alone." Their bright green parakeet hopped to the side of his cage and cocked his head at the flame.

Mr. Pollack gave Jonathan a half smile. "I see you've been expanding Fritzi's vocabulary again. But anyway, I want to hear about your mystery."

Elizabeth and Jonathan described the few clues they had.

"And here's the message. At least what we figured out so far." Elizabeth opened her notebook and held it near the candle.

1879

L. E.

Now i_ __ __m_ to ____ __at ____ lost. Where __ l___

____en I fear __ __y. But t___ m_____g t___ps

___e___r tell the tale. ____em_r

t__ — __o__ have it ____ have it not.

A ____d

"But we're stuck," said Jonathan. "We can't read any more words."

"Call the police!" chimed in Fritzi.

Elizabeth laughed. "Sorry, Fritzi. I don't think the police are interested in a mystery that's over a hundred years old."

Mr. Pollack leaned over the notebook. "I know what's wrong. It's simple. You have to stop looking at the note."

"Stop looking at the note?" Elizabeth shook her head. "How can we read the words if we don't look at the note?"

"I mean you need to concentrate on what you've already figured out. Look at the letters you found, then think of some words that might fit. Later, you can look at the note and see if any of the words match the writing."

"Just think of it like a crossword puzzle," said Mrs. Pollack. "Trying to figure out a word when you only have a few letters. Here, take a look." She moved the candle closer to the notebook. "The message starts with the word *Now*. Then comes a short word beginning with *i*. Probably *is, it*. Something like that."

"But what could this be?" Jonathan pointed to the end of the second sentence: *m_____g t_____ps ___e___r tell the tale.*

Mr. Pollack leaned back in his creaky chair. "Let's see. *Maddening turnips.* Or maybe *marching tulips.*"

"Well, we'll have plenty of time to work on the note," said Mrs. Pollack. "We leave for Maine the day after tomorrow. Three weeks of free time!"

Elizabeth closed the notebook and peeked through the basement window. The rain had stopped, and a thin ray of sunshine poked through the clouds. Across the street she could see her friend Becky in a bright red poncho splashing through puddles. Elizabeth opened the heavy basement door and ran outside. "Becky! We've got a mystery. A real one!"

But the mystery had to wait. Elizabeth knew what was coming. It happened every year. On the day before their trip to Maine, her mother turned into a drill sergeant. Packing suitcases was just the beginning. The house had to be cleaned, the garden weeded, the car washed, the lawn mowed. Elizabeth managed to call Pop in between dusting the piano and folding laundry. But he couldn't help her with the latest clue. The initials *P. R.* meant nothing to him.

Late in the evening, Elizabeth stuffed the last T-shirt into her suitcase. Fritzi watched from his perch on the curtain rod. Just one last thing, thought Elizabeth. Softly, she closed her bedroom door. She slipped her diary into its new hiding place—a pink folder marked World's Best Love Poems. Snoopy Jonathan would never find her journal now. He would rather touch a red hot poker than get near a love poem.

Elizabeth closed her suitcase, then flopped onto the bed. She would miss her room. The low, slanting ceiling and sunny yellow curtains. Fritzi flapped down onto her shoulder. "And I'll miss you too, Fritzi. Even though you listen to Jonathan too much." The parakeet puffed up his feathers. "Call the police," he mumbled. "Girls got cooties."

Mrs. Pollack stuck her head in the door. "You packed your detective notebook, didn't you? And the note?"

"It's right in my backpack, Mom. How come you keep asking?"

"Oh, I can't give away my surprise." Mrs. Pollack gave a mysterious smile. "But I'll tell you one thing. You and Jonathan will get a chance to solve your mystery on this vacation. A chance you never dreamed of."

Unexpected Developments

"Hey, Elizabeth. I found it! The recipe for stir-fried slugs!" Elizabeth leaned against the car window. She squeezed her eyes shut, trying to imagine herself alone on a desert island. It was too much. Her third day in the car, trapped with Jonathan and his favorite book, *The Encyclopedia of the Totally Disgusting.*

Jonathan ran his finger down the table of contents. "We're only on the letter *S.* There's lots more good stuff. *Tongue piercing. Toenails—Legend and Lore.* Then a whole page about warts."

"Mom, can't you do something?"

"Don't worry. We're almost there." They were on a dirt road now, bumping toward a wide grey cottage spread out under the trees. As soon as the car stopped, Elizabeth made her escape. No more back seat. No more stir-fried slugs. She hopped out into a patch of sunlight and twirled herself around. Maine, at last. The air was warm and piney-sweet, filled with summer vacation. The rented cottage looked a little worn and tired, but that didn't matter. The woods were soft and bright. And when Elizabeth stood on tiptoe, she could see a blue sparkle of ocean through the trees.

"Come on, Jon. Let's go check out the house." Elizabeth looked over her shoulder. Jonathan was grunting again, running in circles around a pine tree. "And forget the Outer Mongolian warrior dance!"

Elizabeth edged ahead of Jonathan as they raced inside. "Mom says our room is the one by the kitchen." Elizabeth stopped in the doorway of a large bedroom. Perfect. In one corner stood an important-looking desk. In another, a high cabinet bulged with old board games and jigsaw puzzles.

At first, three weeks seemed like forever. Elizabeth and Jonathan built forts under the pine trees and found a secret path to a long, rocky beach. They finished a jigsaw puzzle—one thousand pieces—and played every board game in the house.

They meant to work on the note again. The shiny red casebook sat ready on the desk, with the old note tucked inside. But somehow the mystery felt far away, like a dim light in the distance. Elizabeth even stopped wondering about her mother's mysterious secret. Then, on the last day of their vacation, Shipwreck Cove changed everything.

Jonathan had looked at a map on the kitchen wall. "Mom, didn't you want to see that place called Shipwreck Cove? Where the lighthouse is?"

They set out just after dinner, snaking along the coast on a lonely two-lane road. Elizabeth spotted Shipwreck Cove just around a curve. It was a rough, pebbly bit of beach, with a rocky finger of land stretching out to sea. At the very tip, a sleek white lighthouse held on to the last glow of sunshine.

The others headed toward the water, but Elizabeth sat down at the grassy edge of the beach. The stones were dry there, still warm from the afternoon sun. Elizabeth let a lazy stream of pebbles run through her fingers. Then something caught her eye—bits of glass, rounded smooth by the sea. Green. Pink. A hazy shade of purple. She picked through the stones and gathered the glass in her hand.

The beach was all shadow now. Elizabeth shivered at the cold sound of waves slapping the rocks. Shipwreck Cove. What if the glass came from sunken ships? She picked up a tiny piece of china, still faintly showing one delicate pink rose. The little flower seemed out of place here, all alone among the speckled stones and sharp bits of shell. It could have been part of a plate once. Or maybe someone's cup.

Suddenly she scrambled to her feet and ran toward the others. "Teacups! It's teacups!"

"It's what?" Jonathan was bent over a crab. He didn't look up.

Elizabeth leaned down and traced letters into the wet sand. *t____ps* "Don't you remember? One of the missing words from the old note begins with *t* and ends with *ps*. It's *teacups*. I know it is."

Mr. Pollack stood next to her and traced more letters into the sand. *m____g* "*Matching*," he said. "It could be *matching teacups*."

Jonathan shook his head. "No way. Why would someone write a note about teacups?"

"There's only one way to find out," said Mrs. Pollack. "Let's get back and take a look at the note."

It was dark by the time they reached the cottage. Jonathan fumbled for the light switch, then rushed through the kitchen and into the bedroom. Holding a small magnifying glass, he set the note on the pale wood of the old desk.

"This is really weird, Elizabeth. I think you're right!" Jonathan handed her the magnifying glass. She could see the tip of a *t* and an *h* in the first word, the curve of a *c* and a *u* in the second. The words *matching teacups* were a perfect fit. But what did it mean?

1879

L. E.
Now i_ __ _m_ to _____ __at _____ lost. Where __ l___
_____en I fear __ __y. But t___ matching teacups ____e___r
tell the tale. _____em_r
t__— __o__ have it _____ have it not.

A _____d

Elizabeth opened the red detective notebook. "Okay, Jon. Let's get going. Dad was right. First we look at the blanks and think of words that might fit. Then we'll look at the old note and see if any of the words match."

Mr. Pollack appeared in the doorway. "Sorry. Not tonight. We're leaving early tomorrow morning. You two need to start packing your things. And no arguments."

Mrs. Pollack called out from the living room. "Tomorrow night you can work on the note. At the motel."

"But, Mom." Elizabeth shuffled out of the bedroom. "Could you at least call Pop and ask him if he knows anything about teacups?"

Jonathan handed his mother the telephone. "And if Aunt Marie is there, don't talk to her forever. Please." He folded his arms for emphasis. Mrs. Pollack's conversations with her sister could last for hours.

Elizabeth smiled as she plopped an armload of clothes into her suitcase. She had no trouble overhearing the phone call. Her mother's voice began softly, then swelled to full volume. It was a sure sign she was talking to Pop.

"We figured out another word from the note. We found the word *teacups* in the message." Mrs. Pollack's voice went up a notch. "Not *sea pups*, Dad. *Tea-cups*." There was a pause.

"I'm not mumbling. And I didn't say *teeth*. I said *tea*. *Tea-cups*." Her voice rose to a near yell.

She walked into their room a few minutes later. "Sorry, kids. Pop did finally understand me, but he doesn't remember anything about teacups. Maybe you'll get more ideas when you figure out the rest of the note."

Elizabeth lay awake long after the lights were out. Jonathan was right. A note written about teacups didn't seem at all mysterious. But if there was no mystery, why was the note hidden? And the words on the frame. *P. R. did it. the thirteenth.*

Elizabeth turned away from the cool night air creeping in through the window. She felt lonely, staring into the darkness while the rest of the family slept. She reached down and pulled the soft blanket tight against her chin. Tomorrow, she thought. Tomorrow night they would work on the note and not go to sleep until they figured out the secret message. Every word.

Early the next morning, Elizabeth and Jonathan half dozed through the first hour in the car. After one last bright glimpse of ocean, a wide and busy highway took them away from the sea. They drove with few stops, always farther west. By the end of the day Elizabeth sat grimly in the back seat, trying to forget the soggy hamburger she ate for dinner.

"I'd like to get farther into New York," said Mr. Pollack. "It's only seven o'clock. I think we could go another eighty miles." Another eighty miles? Elizabeth couldn't believe what she was hearing. She needed a long evening, with plenty of time to work on the note. "But, Dad, we have to . . ." Elizabeth stiffened suddenly and wrinkled her nose. A peculiar odor was filling the car, getting stronger by the minute. It smelled like fish. Rotten fish.

Elizabeth and her mother turned their eyes on Jonathan, suspect number one. He sat chuckling over *The Encyclopedia of the Totally Disgusting*. A stink bomb, decided Elizabeth. The book probably gave him the recipe.

Jonathan looked up. "How come I get blamed for everything? I don't know where the smell is coming from!" He picked up a small bucket with a plastic lid. "I mean, it can't be my shells. They smell good. Like seaweed. Here, I'll show you." He pried open the bucket and held it under his sister's nose. The stench from the unrinsed shells rose up like an evil genie. Elizabeth swatted the bucket away. "Seaweed? You mean seaweed that's been rotting for a thousand years!" She grabbed the back of the driver's seat. "We can't keep driving, Dad! Those shells—they're making me sick!"

Jonathan's eyes lit up. "Medical emergency! Abandon ship! Lower the lifeboats!"

"Oh, come on," said Mr. Pollack. "Look at it scientifically. The organic matter in the shells is breaking down. We just need to add a little vinegar. The chemical reaction gets rid of the smell."

Mrs. Pollack rolled down her window. "Well, we don't have any vinegar, and we can't go on like this. We've got to look for a motel." Elizabeth smiled. Her mother's tone left no room for discussion.

"What about that place?" Jonathan pointed ahead to a slender red-brick house. Next to the shiny black door was a brass sign. BED

AND BREAKFAST. Soon they were settled into a bright room overlooking the garden.

"Now, this is the spot for a weary traveler." Mrs. Pollack followed the others down the stairs into a roomy parlor. A soft scent of roses drifted in through the window. Taking a fat leather book from a shelf near the fireplace, she sat down on the sofa next to Mr. Pollack.

"And just the right place for working on our mystery." Elizabeth walked up to a wide, round table by the window. She patted the bottom of the thick wooden legs. "It even has feet. Like lion's paws." She set her red notebook on the dark tabletop and took out the note. Jonathan's voice bubbled in from the hallway. He was having a lively talk with the woman who owned the inn.

A moment later he rushed through the door. "The lady put some vinegar on my shells. And look what she gave me! She said they use it for their stamp collection." He held a heavy round magnifying glass above the note. The letters swelled up thick and large, as if they would pop off the page.

"Perfect. Let's get to work." Elizabeth helped Jonathan drag two heavy chairs to the table. Jonathan picked up the magnifying glass. "Not yet, Jon. We still can't see all the letters. We have to think of words that might fit the blanks."

The first missing word took exactly two minutes. Jonathan looked at their list. "A short word beginning with *i*, like *is*, *if*, *it* or *it's*." He squinted through the thick lens. "Easy! It has to be *is*. I can see a little squiggle, like the top of an *s*."

Elizabeth read the first two words of the note. "*Now is . . .*" She tapped her finger on the table. "Then comes a short word. *The*. It could be the word *the*!" Suddenly they seemed to have a magic key, opening up one secret after another. The more words they figured out, the faster they found the next. The first sentence was done, then the second and the third. It was easy now, like riding a bicycle downhill.

"We did it!" Jonathan popped out of his chair. Mr. and Mrs. Pollack put their books down and came over to the table.

"Don't look yet! Let me read it to you." Elizabeth stood up by the window. "I'm going to—" She stepped back. The gauzy white curtain next to her billowed up on a sudden wind. It floated toward her, swaying like a ghost.

She looked down at the note. Grandma Lydia must have held it, just like this, over one hundred years ago. Elizabeth read the words out loud, trying to keep her hand from trembling.

1879

L. E.
Now is the time to find what was lost. Where it lies hidden I fear to say. But two matching teacups together tell the tale. Remember this—you have it yet have it not.
A Friend

Mrs. Pollack was the first to speak. She took the note from Elizabeth. "So Grandma Lydia lost something. But how?"

Elizabeth thought about the words on the picture frame. She thought about Mr. Lattimore, sitting on the creaky chair in his shop. *I think we've stumbled onto the traces of crime*, he had said. *A crime committed a long time ago.* Elizabeth turned to her mother. "When the note says *lost*, I think it means stolen. Something was stolen from Grandma Lydia. And then hidden. And the initials of the thief are *P. R.*" Elizabeth glanced at her father. He stood by the fireplace with a doubtful frown. His scientist look, she called it. "And don't say it's just my imagination, Dad. *P. R. did it.* That's what was written on the frame. He was probably a thief or a robber. And mean too. That's why the person writing the note was afraid to tell about the hiding place."

"An interesting . . . theory," said Mr. Pollack. "But we do know one thing for sure. Something was hidden, and Grandma Lydia was supposed to find it."

Jonathan sat slumped in his chair. "Wait a minute. I don't get it. The words sound so weird. Matching teacups telling a tale. How can teacups tell a story?"

"The person who wrote the note was probably afraid to say very much," said Mrs. Pollack. "So the note isn't too clear. It's more like a code that has to be figured out. Here, I'll read it again: *Now is the time to find what was lost. Where it lies hidden I fear to say. But two matching teacups together tell the tale. Remember this—you have it yet have it not. A Friend.*"

Jonathan leaned forward as he listened. "Now I get it! The note says two teacups tell a tale. So that means there's a clue in the teacups, and the clue tells where to find the thing that was hidden."

"That's it, Jon!" Elizabeth grinned. "A clue in the teacups. Something was stolen, and a clue in the teacups tells where it is. Not bad for an eight-year-old." She stood next to her mother. "The only thing is, how could we ever find the clue? I mean, where would we find teacups that were around in 1879?"

"Well . . ." Mrs. Pollack let the word hang in the air. Then she smiled. The very same way she smiled on the night before their trip.

Elmwood House

"You're not moving an inch!" Elizabeth steered her mother into a plump brown armchair by the fireplace.

Jonathan stood guard with his arms crossed. "Not 'til you tell us the secret."

"Okay, I give up!" Mrs. Pollack leaned her head against the back of the chair. "Here it is. At this time tomorrow night, you two ace detectives will be investigating Grandma Lydia's parlor."

"But I don't get it." Elizabeth dropped onto the sofa next to her father. "Pop's grandmother died a long time ago!"

"That's right," said Mr. Pollack. "But her house is still standing. And some of Mom's relatives live there. It's in Ohio, right on our way home. We'll be staying overnight."

"You mean the house Pop told us about?" Jonathan leaped in front of the armchair. "With the gloomy parlor? Where the fortune-teller clock used to be?"

"Exactly. It's called Elmwood House. My Uncle Richard lives there. Pop's brother. He and Aunt Doris have been fixing up the place." Mrs. Pollack gazed at the old note in her hand. "Just like it was in Grandma Lydia's day. As if the house is waiting for us. And who knows? Maybe those mysterious teacups are waiting there too."

Elizabeth sat very still, watching the white curtain gently rise and fall on the breeze. She had a strange, faraway feeling. It was like floating backwards down a river. Straight into the past.

They set out just after breakfast the next day. New York was soon behind them, but Pennsylvania seemed as big as an ocean. It was late afternoon by the time the hills melted away. They had reached the heart of Ohio, stretched out wide and flat as an open book.

"It won't be long now. We're already past Columbus." Mrs. Pollack unfolded a large map. "I can't wait until my Uncle Richard hears about your mystery. He's interested in family history, you know. Just like Pop."

"Uh, speaking of Pop," said Jonathan. "Since Uncle Richard is his brother . . . I mean, is he like Pop? Kind of loud and grumpy?"

"Not a bit. He's very friendly and easygoing. Of course, you could say he's a little . . . oh, I don't know—unusual."

"Unusual?" Elizabeth looked at Jonathan. It must run in the family.

"Well, unusual in a good way. You see, my Uncle Richard is interested in just about everything. I always picture him sitting at his kitchen table, reading the encyclopedia. He reads it cover to cover, like a chapter book. Marie and I used to call him Uncle Questions." Mrs. Pollack ran her finger along the map. "Anyway, in a little while you can see for yourselves."

Elizabeth soon gave up looking out the window. The highway ran straight as a needle past mounds of soybeans and stiff rows of corn. She couldn't imagine secrets here, with the land so neat and flat and open to the sky.

"Hey, Elizabeth! I know how long it takes for a dead worm to decompose." Elizabeth narrowed her eyes at Jonathan. Maybe *The Encyclopedia of the Totally Disgusting* would decompose. It could be buried in a deep hole. A very deep hole. "Jonathan, can't you just . . . hey, Dad! How come we're stopping?" They were off the busy highway now, pulled over on a narrow, patched-up road. Elizabeth could see an overgrown field, and in the middle, a small white house. "But this can't be Elmwood House. It's empty!"

Mr. Pollack turned off the motor. "Surprise number two. Diamond Prairie Farm."

"Diamond what?" Elizabeth pushed up her glasses and peered out the window. The house didn't look like diamond anything. It was a tiny, tumble-down place, slouched in the tall grass like a tattered old hat.

"Diamond Prairie Farm," said Mrs. Pollack. "I thought you'd want to see this. You see, Joshua Bailey gave this little farmhouse to Grandma Lydia right after she married Thomas Emerson. I think they lived here for about twenty years. That was before they bought Elmwood House."

Jonathan closed his book. "You mean Grandma Lydia had two houses? And this was the first one?"

"Right," said Mrs. Pollack. "This is where they started out. Thomas Emerson was a carpenter. His workshop was in the barn. And they raised cows too. And sheep."

"So if Grandma Lydia lived here for twenty years after she got married, that means . . ." Elizabeth grabbed her red notebook and turned to the page of dates. "Grandma Lydia was living in this house in 1879. When she got the note!"

Jonathan hopped out of the car. "So the stolen treasure might be hidden right here!"

"But . . ." Mr. Pollack put his hand on Elizabeth's arm. "I don't want you to get your hopes up about treasure. We have no idea what was hidden."

"I know, Dad. But it has to be something valuable. I mean, if someone just hid a pen or something, people wouldn't be writing secret notes about it."

Mrs. Pollack picked up her camera. "Well, I guess we don't need scientific proof for everything. How about this? Dad and I want to take some pictures. You two can hunt for your treasure."

"Hey, wait up, Jon!" Elizabeth hurried along a knobby stone fence that ran beside the road. Jonathan stood in an opening marked by two small pillars. Each was half hidden under a tangle of vines.

"This will be my first picture. You two stand right here." Mrs. Pollack arranged them next to the pillars then snapped a picture. "You can go in the house if you're careful. Try the back door. The last time I was here it was unlocked."

Jonathan stood at the edge of the field. "I bet snakes live in there. Lots of them."

"Right. Thanks, Jon." Elizabeth looked down at the bare toes sticking out of her sandals. Suddenly the house looked a long way off. "Okay. Here goes." She plunged into the field, holding out her detective notebook like a shield. The tall grass was scratchy and dry, popping with grasshoppers. She and Jonathan waded their way to a rickety square of back porch. The rough wooden door was already open a crack. Elizabeth gave a timid push, then took one step into a dim, narrow kitchen.

"Wait, Jon. Don't move!" Elizabeth closed her eyes. A scent hung in the air. Only for a moment. Then it was gone, disappearing in a hot smell of dust and old wallpaper. Elizabeth opened her notebook and clicked her green pen. *Diamond Prairie Farm. Smelled something sharp and sweet. Men's cologne?* Elizabeth looked around the empty kitchen. It was stripped as bare as a bone, except for a grimy sink full of dead moths. "Jon, I can smell some kind of perfume. Like someone's been here."

"Well, I don't smell anything. And don't close your eyes and go into one of those trances."

Jonathan crunched across a pile of fallen plaster and squatted in front of a low cabinet with no door. "Hey! There's a nest in here." He stood up with a grin. "Probably rats."

"Jonathan, can't you think about anything except rats and snakes and dead worms?" Elizabeth turned away and walked through an open doorway to another empty room. "I guess this was the living room." She bent over a broken stub of broom propped up in a rusty bucket. A yellow scrap of newspaper lay underneath. "Look at this date, Jon. I don't think anyone has lived here for twenty years."

Elizabeth brushed past a strip of flowered wallpaper, drooping down like a half peeled banana. Everything in the room seemed dry and brittle, like an old leaf about to crumble. And so hot. She longed to open all the windows, let the wind breathe some life into the house.

Jonathan clanked around in a small room on the other side of the kitchen. "We could still find clues, you know. A secret hiding place or something." They moved through the house slowly, pounding and pushing and prying. They searched three rooms downstairs, then a small loft with chinks of sky showing through the roof. After fifteen minutes they had collected three bent nails and the top of a spaghetti jar.

"I guess that's it." Elizabeth made one more slow circle in the living room. She tried to imagine Grandma Lydia here. She could have read the note in this very room. By the window maybe. Or by the light of a . . . "Jonathan, what's wrong with you? You're looking at me like I just grew fangs!"

Jonathan stood stiff as a post. "Turn around." He didn't say the words. He just formed them with his mouth.

"Quit trying to scare me." Elizabeth glanced over her shoulder, then nearly stumbled as she backed away from the window. A face was pressed against the dirty glass. Bushy grey beard. A nose as sharp as an ax. It looked like . . . the painting at Pop's house. As if Joshua Bailey had just stepped out of his portrait.

The old man's lips moved. He yelled something. Something that sounded like, *What's the capital of Albania?* Elizabeth looked at Jonathan. Uncle Questions. It had to be.

She ran out the back door and waved with her red notebook. "Tirana. The capital of Albania is Tirana."

"And you're Uncle Richard." Jonathan peeked out the back door.

Uncle Richard hopped up on the porch. He was lean as a shipwrecked sailor, with a face all beard and wrinkles. For some reason Elizabeth could picture him with a parrot on his shoulder.

"You two are smart ones. Just like your mother." One straggly eyebrow shot up when he smiled. "Now here's another question. The hissing cockroach comes from what island nation?"

"Madagascar!" Mrs. Pollack came up from behind and hugged her uncle. Elizabeth shook her head. Talk about strange greetings.

"How did you know we were here?" asked Mr. Pollack.

"I spotted your car on my way home from the store." Uncle Richard's smile faded. "I'm glad you came to see the old place. I'm afraid it won't be around much longer. You see, no one wants to rent the house. A cousin of mine owns it, but she doesn't think it's worth fixing up."

"But they can't let the house fall apart," said Jonathan. "It's part of our mystery."

"Your mystery?" Uncle Richard's eyebrow was on the move again. "I like the sound of that!"

"It's about your grandmother Lydia," said Elizabeth. "She hid a note behind an old painting of her father."

"Yeah. And we're looking for treasure! Stolen treasure!"

"Hold on, you two." Mr. Pollack pulled the back door shut. "Let's get to Elmwood House first. Then we can tell Uncle Richard and Aunt Doris all about it."

"Follow me, then. I'll take you the back way." Uncle Richard climbed into a boxy blue car that looked just like Pop's. He drove slowly through a maze of narrow roads, waving into the rearview mirror each time he turned. Before long a little town popped up from the flat fields. It wasn't much, just two blocks of stores huddled around a sturdy red-brick bank.

Uncle Richard turned left at the only stoplight. He pulled up to a stately house, shaded by two tall, straight trees. Elizabeth didn't have to ask. Elmwood House was just as she imagined—graceful and creamy white, with big windows and a wide, lazy front porch. Elizabeth opened her notebook and ran her hand over the old yellowed note. They were meant to be at this house. She was sure of it.

Uncle Richard jumped out of his car and waited for them on the front steps. "*Ulmus americana!*" His index finger quivered in the air. "Who can tell me the common name of this well-known shade tree?"

"Elm!" Jonathan picked up a stick and made two turns around the tree.

"Correct! American elm, to be exact. Coarsely double-toothed leaves, upper surface smooth to the touch. Threatened, unfortunately, by Dutch elm disease." Uncle Richard swung open the wide wooden door. "Welcome to Elmwood House."

They followed him into a large front hall with a shiny wooden floor. A tall grandfather clock, straight and solemn as a butler, chimed six o'clock.

"My word, it's been a long time." A stout, soft-looking woman came out of the kitchen, patting down her dark grey curls. She was only a bit taller than Elizabeth. "I'm your Great-aunt Doris." She reached out a puffy hand and gently squeezed Elizabeth's arm. "I hope Richard hasn't been exhausting you with questions."

She saw Jonathan stretching his neck toward the kitchen. "And I hope you like chicken and mashed potatoes. With blueberry pie and ice cream for dessert."

Jonathan closed his eyes. "I'm in heaven."

"It'll just be a few more minutes," said Aunt Doris. "Richard, why don't you show them the parlor? They've never seen the renovations."

"Yeah, we know about the parlor," said Jonathan. "Pop told us how spooky it used to be. With sheets over the furniture and everything."

Uncle Richard grinned. "Well, we tried to make the room just like it used to be. But without the sheets." He turned around and slid open a heavy wooden door.

The old parlor appeared before them, silent and still, like a stage set for a play. Elizabeth tiptoed into the room, moving step by step into Grandma Lydia's world. It was a dainty and proper place. Green velvet chairs with thin, curved legs. Squares of white lace on the tables. And a comfortable smell of wax and old wood. Like a museum. Elizabeth could almost hear whispery, long-ago voices. The ladies would be in long, high-necked dresses, sitting up very straight and never spilling anything.

"I'm a better detective than you are." Jonathan gave Elizabeth a sharp poke in the ribs. He hurled himself onto the flowered carpet and rolled into a somersault.

"Jonathan, what are you babbling about?" Elizabeth glanced at the grown-ups clustered around an old rolltop desk. "And quit rolling around on the floor. You're acting like a two-year-old."

"I'm not babbling." Jonathan sat up and jutted his chin in Elizabeth's direction. "I *am* a better detective than you. 'Cause I found the teacups, and you didn't."

Another Message

Elizabeth caught Jonathan by the sleeve as he scrambled to his feet. "What are you talking about? I don't see any . . ." She let go of his T-shirt. She did see something now. Next to the prim velvet sofa was a small, three-legged table. Elizabeth moved forward, not daring to blink. On the table was a blue and white teapot. And two matching teacups.

"Now that's what I like to see! Young people interested in porcelain!" Uncle Richard hurried over with Mr. and Mrs. Pollack. He picked up one of the cups, pinching the curly handle between his thumb and index finger. The teacup was delicate and fine, covered with pictures in Elizabeth's favorite shade of blue. A strong, deep blue, like the ocean on a bright summer morning.

"This is a Chinese pattern," said Uncle Richard. "Blue Willow. It's been popular for years." Elizabeth leaned closer. The cup was like a little painting. A pair of tiny birds soared in the air above pagodas and bridges and willow trees. A wide band of triangles decorated the top. Elizabeth frowned suddenly. The teacup looked as frail as an eggshell. How could it be over a hundred years old?

"Uncle Richard? This cup. Was it around in 1879? I mean, did it belong to your grandmother Lydia?"

"Grandma Lydia? Well, yes. Yes, it did. My parents had the tea set packed away at their house in Oklahoma. Originally it belonged to my grandparents though." Elizabeth looked at her mother and relaxed into a smile. *Two matching teacups together tell the tale.* And now they had them.

Uncle Richard picked up the second cup. "And here's my lucky find. I bought it just last month at an antique shop. You see, one of the original cups was lost. But this one is quite similar. It's just . . . Is something wrong?"

"There's . . . only one cup." Elizabeth drew back, as if a door had slammed in her face. She could see now. The second cup was wider. The birds were more plump, and the trees . . . Everything was different.

"But how did it get lost?" Jonathan's voice sounded small.

"I don't know, really. There used to be two cups. I'm sure of it. But when I unpacked the box, I found only one." Uncle Richard set the cup back down in its saucer. "Does this by any chance have to do with your mystery?"

Mrs. Pollack looked up as Aunt Doris announced dinner. "I'm afraid it does. And it's quite a story."

Elizabeth sat beside Jonathan at a long, dark table in the dining room. She took a little bit of everything, just to be polite. But she wasn't hungry. It wasn't fair. They had figured out the note, come all this way. And now they only had one teacup.

Elizabeth and Jonathan poured out the whole story. The portrait of Joshua Bailey. The old note. The words on the frame: *P. R. did it* and *the thirteenth.*

Elizabeth opened her notebook. "And this is the note we told you about. We figured out all the words. Just last night."

Uncle Richard's fork clattered onto his plate. "But this is a real mystery! I thought you were just playing some detective game because . . . it's just strange. Grandma Lydia never told us anything about a crime. And she was always telling family stories."

"I know it's hard to believe," said Mr. Pollack. "But we think . . .

Well, we can't prove it, but we think a person with the initials *P. R.* stole something from your grandmother. And then someone wrote this note, telling about a clue in the teacups that would lead her to the hiding place."

Uncle Richard leaned over and squinted at the note.

"Here, I'll read it to you," said Elizabeth. "I know it by heart." She stood next to Uncle Richard, pointing to the words as she read.

"*L. E. Now is the time to find what was lost. Where it lies hidden I fear to say. But two matching teacups together tell the tale. Remember this— you have it yet have it not.* And at the bottom it says, *A Friend.*"

"So you need both cups," said Aunt Doris. "Both cups together to find the clue."

Uncle Richard rubbed his hand over his forehead. "I wish I could help you, but I just don't know where that other cup is. You see, I packed up the tea set years ago, when my mother moved out of her

house in Oklahoma. I didn't unpack it until a few months ago. I suppose Pop could have the other cup. He was with me when we sorted out mother's things. Of course, it may be that the cup was broken or lost."

"Well, I wouldn't give up." Aunt Doris touched Elizabeth's hand softly. "That other cup might turn up somewhere. And I've always had . . . I don't know . . . a feeling that this old house still has some secrets to tell."

After dinner Elizabeth stood alone in the parlor, holding Grandma Lydia's teacup. Slowly she turned the cup in the palm of her hand. Chinese pagodas. Bridges. Soaring birds. What did they have to do with a theft from her great-great-grandmother?

"How about joining us in the sitting room, Elizabeth? Your mother and father went out for a walk." Uncle Richard poked his head into the doorway.

Elizabeth followed him into a small, cluttered room at the front of the house. Jonathan was already there, winding up a yo-yo. Aunt Doris was curled up on a puffy brown couch with a newspaper crossword puzzle. "Careful you don't trip over Richard's books." Elizabeth stepped over three stacks of books and sank into a wide armchair.

Uncle Richard pointed to the red notebook in her lap. "Your mother tells me you like to write."

"Yeah. Elizabeth writes stuff all the time." Jonathan yanked his yo-yo up and down. "She has this diary and she tries to hide it. But I always find it. And she writes about how she—ouch!" Elizabeth had struck as quick as a snake. She caught the fleshy part of Jonathan's arm, just above the elbow.

Uncle Richard cleared his throat. "Well, I'm sure you're a fine writer." He stood in front of a small fireplace and patted down his beard. "Question! What's the name for the system that helped runaway slaves escape to freedom?"

"The Underground Railroad," said Elizabeth. "We learned about it in school this year."

"Exactly. Here, let me show you something." Uncle Richard

opened the glass doors of a high bookcase. "You see, Grandma Lydia liked to write too." He pulled out a thin notebook with a cover of faded green paper. "I found this up in the attic. It's a history of the Bailey family, written by Grandma Lydia. She used to read it to me when I was a boy. If it weren't for this little book, we'd know almost nothing about the family."

"But what about the Underground Railroad?"

Uncle Richard gently turned the thin pages. "Well, you probably don't know this, but one of our ancestors owned slaves. He was a ship-builder out East. That was way back in the 1700s, when slavery was still legal in Massachusetts."

"Owned . . . slaves?" Elizabeth stared at the green notebook.

"I'm afraid so. But later, someone else in the family helped slaves who were escaping from the South. Grandma Lydia had an Aunt Samantha who lived in Boston. According to this family history, Samantha Bailey's house was on the Underground Railroad. She had a secret room behind a bookcase. That's where the slaves hid."

Jonathan skipped over to Uncle Richard. "I read a story like that! With a hidden room and everything."

"Richard and I are going to do some detective work," said Aunt Doris. "We've done a lot of research on the Underground Railroad in Boston. We're going there next spring to see if we can find the house. And that secret room." She set her newspaper on the table. "But my very special dream is to go to Ireland. Find the village where my grandparents came from. You know, there's nothing like family history if you like puzzles."

"And mysteries," said Elizabeth softly. She stood up and gazed at the notebook in Uncle Richard's hands. The handwriting was careful and pretty, with fancy capital letters that looped and curled like wisps of smoke. "Did Grandma Lydia write about something being stolen?"

"No. She didn't write about a theft. Unless . . . Wait a minute!" Uncle Richard's dark eyes lit up like a match. "I do remember seeing something . . . something strange written in this book. It was a long time ago. Just a couple of sentences I didn't understand. Now where was that?" He held a page toward the window to catch the last bit of daylight. Two lines of small letters were squeezed at the bottom of the last page. "Here. Listen to what she wrote. *I shall not speak of that terrible night. Those who find the note must try to set things right.*"

Slowly, Uncle Richard turned to Jonathan and Elizabeth. "Grandma Lydia was writing about the two of you. *Those who find the note.*"

"You mean, me and Elizabeth?" Jonathan stood with his yo-yo dangling.

"I don't know why Grandma Lydia never told us about this mystery," said Uncle Richard. "But she knew that someone in the future would find that note. Someone like you. She wants you to set things right—find the clue in the teacups and get back what was stolen." Uncle Richard paced a circle around Elizabeth and Jonathan. "She's working with you, leaving clues. The writing on the picture frame. And the words she said just before she died. It's . . ." Uncle Richard stood still. His grey eyebrows floated upwards, making his eyes seem twice as big. "It's like a voice from beyond the grave."

Aunt Doris gently pulled him onto the couch next to her. "Now, Richard. Don't get overdramatic. You'll frighten the children."

Elizabeth dropped back into the armchair. She felt shivery, as if an icy drop of water were dripping down her back. A few weeks ago, she knew nothing about her great-great-grandmother. But now everything was different. Something happened, long ago on a terrible night. And Elizabeth had to find out what. "We want to solve the mystery. But we don't have the second teacup. And we don't even know what was stolen. Or how." Elizabeth blinked into the room. She hadn't noticed the sunlight slipping away, but now the edges of things were getting fuzzy, melting into shadow. Elizabeth could hear the grandfather clock in the front hall, ticking slowly, patiently. As if it were trying to tell them something. She straightened up in her chair.

"If Grandma Lydia wanted us to solve the mystery, she would have told us more. I mean, left another clue around here somewhere."

"Another clue? But where?" Uncle Richard shook his head.

"We've redone the house from top to bottom. Except the stairway and . . . Well, there's the attic. We've never done anything with the attic."

"And Grandma Lydia's papers are up there somewhere," said Aunt Doris. "We put the papers from her desk in a box."

"Anybody here?" Elizabeth jumped at the sound of her father's deep voice. She could see a tall shadow standing in the doorway to the sitting room.

"Hmm. Looks spooky in here." Mrs. Pollack appeared from the front hall and felt her way into the room. "You must be discussing the mystery."

Aunt Doris clicked on a small table lamp. "We certainly were. You see, we've just found another message from Grandma Lydia."

The new clue was discussed until Aunt Doris noticed Jonathan asleep in the corner of the sofa. "Ten o'clock? How did it get this late? I'd better show you where you'll be sleeping." Aunt Doris climbed up the wide front stairway, leaning heavily on the banister. "Your bedroom is here, Elizabeth. Right at the top of the stairs."

In a few minutes Elizabeth was settled into a narrow, high bed. She wondered if Grandma Lydia had ever slept in this room, had ever watched lightning bugs glowing in the elm tree just outside the window.

"Mom, I was just thinking." Elizabeth made room for her mother on the edge of the bed. "Pop and Uncle Richard know so much about the family, and I hardly know anything."

"Well, Pop and Uncle Richard are memory keepers. That's what I call them. You see, they save pieces of the past."

"You mean, like the fortune-teller clock Pop has? And the old portrait?"

"That's right. But they save stories, too. Funny stories and sad stories. And stories about things you read in history books. Sometimes you forget that people in your own family *lived* that history." Mrs. Pollack brushed Elizabeth's forehead with a kiss. "The trouble is, usually no one takes the time to listen to the stories. Then they just disappear. Like a gift no one wants."

"Jonathan and I are going to be memory keepers." Elizabeth sank into the pillow. It felt soft and smelled faintly of rose petals. "And I'm going to write things down, just like Grandma Lydia did. But first, we have to solve this mystery."

Elizabeth's eyes fell shut as soon as the hall light went off. Grandma Lydia must have left one more clue. One more. The attic. Tomorrow.

Exploring the Attic

Elizabeth snapped awake, her eyes wide open in the deep, middle-of-the-night darkness. Something—a noise, not a dream—had startled her from her sleep. A long, sharp creaking on the front stairway. Tense and alert, she lay still, straining her ears, but she heard nothing more. She floated back to sleep on the gentle ticking of the grandfather clock. Strange, she thought. A creak on the stairs but no footsteps.

In the morning, a patch of sunlight snuggled like a cat at the foot of the bed. Elizabeth was glad for the brightness, and for the flowered curtains and the honey color of the wooden floor. She was in her great-great-grandmother's house. And this was the day they would look for clues in the attic.

"Sorry. I guess I'm the last one up." Elizabeth had found a steep back stairway leading to the kitchen. The others sat at a round table, busy with scrambled eggs and blueberry muffins.

Uncle Richard jumped up and made room for another chair. "We were just discussing the encyclopedia. Volume H. One of my favorites." He pointed to a thick book propped up next to his coffee cup. "By the way, the ancestors of the modern American horse were brought from what country?"

"Spain," laughed Elizabeth. "I've read millions of books about horses." She slipped into a chair next to her mother. Mrs. Pollack winked at her.

"Correct! And one more. True or false? The earliest horses were as small as cats."

"Richard! Please! You let Elizabeth eat her breakfast." Aunt Doris set the basket of muffins next to Elizabeth's plate.

"I just asked Uncle Richard about ghosts." Jonathan jabbed into a mountain of scrambled eggs. "'Cause old houses always have ghosts."

"There *was* some story, wasn't there?" asked Mrs. Pollack. "Something about a sound of crying."

"Oh, this house has a story all right." Uncle Richard pushed aside his empty plate. "It's . . . It's about the bedroom where you slept, Elizabeth. I'm not sure you want to hear it. Doris says I get carried away with stories."

"That's okay. I don't believe in ghosts. They're not . . ." Elizabeth looked at her father. "They're not scientific."

Uncle Richard folded his thin hands on the edge of the table. "Well, all right. You see, this house was built way back in 1850. So it was already old when my grandparents bought it. The first owner was a Mrs. Nesbit. Elma Nesbit, I believe. She warned Grandma Lydia never to use that front room upstairs as a bedroom. She said whoever slept there would hear things during the night. It always started the same. A creaking stair. No sound of footsteps. Just a creak on the front stairway."

Elizabeth didn't look up. She kept her eyes on the edge of butter melting into her muffin. *No sound of footsteps. Just a creak on the front stairway.*

"It would happen during the darkest part of night." Uncle Richard was crouched forward now, his long beard skimming the table. "First the creaking, then the sound of someone sobbing. One night Mrs. Nesbit lit a candle and got out of bed. When she started walking down the stairs, something reached out from the darkness and grabbed her arm. It was a hand. A woman's hand, she said, as cold and white as the moon. Mrs. Nesbit ran back up the stairs and spent the rest of the night locked in another bedroom. She never slept in the front room again. But for the rest of her life she had a pale spot on her arm. The spot where the white hand had touched her."

Elizabeth sent the clump of muffin down with one hard swallow. The creak on the stairs during the night. It must have been Uncle Richard or Aunt Doris going downstairs. But somehow she didn't want to ask. What if they said no?

Aunt Doris got up and swung open the back door. "My land! It does get hot in this kitchen. It's going to be a scorcher today." She smiled at Elizabeth. "Now, remember. That's just a story. We've never heard any sobbing ghosts in the house. And lots of people have slept in that room."

"But the stair. Does it still creak?"

"Oh, yes," said Uncle Richard. "That stair has creaked for almost a hundred and fifty years."

After breakfast, Elizabeth followed Uncle Richard and Jonathan up the back stairs. "Wait for me. I'll be right back." Elizabeth hurried to the end of the long hallway, keeping her eyes away from the front stairway. She ran into her room and grabbed her red detective notebook from the night table. The mystery. She had to get her mind back on the mystery.

"The attic is right through here." Uncle Richard led them into a tiny room with an oversized desk. In the corner, a narrow white door led to seven wooden steps. Elizabeth climbed up slowly, pressing into the thick, hot air. The attic was small and low, nothing like the bright and polished rooms downstairs. It was the skeleton of the house, with dark beams and rough boards slanting up to the roof. On the far wall, one round window let in a weak drizzle of daylight.

"Hey, Uncle Richard, what's this?" Jonathan stood in the corner, next to an old Western saddle balanced between two chairs.

"That's my father's saddle. He used it only with Button, his favorite horse. Your grandfather and I used to ride him too."

"Pop? He used to ride horses?"

"Oh, sure, he was quite a rider. We grew up on a cattle ranch in Oklahoma." Uncle Richard let his hand glide along the curve of dark leather. "Pop was even a teacher in a one-room schoolhouse for awhile. I imagine he's told you all the stories."

"Well, not exactly." Elizabeth tried to picture Pop's face. All she came up with was a scowl behind a haze of cigar smoke. "Pop doesn't tell many stories. He thinks kids are interested only in stuff like video games and TV."

"Sounds to me like he's waiting for you to ask him." Uncle Richard turned toward the stairway. "Anyway, I'll let you two do some exploring on your own. Those papers from Grandma Lydia's desk are up here somewhere. I've looked through them a few times. Never noticed anything unusual." He leaned forward with a smile. "But two fine detectives like you might find an important clue."

Jonathan wandered to the back of the attic. Elizabeth watched Uncle Richard disappear down the stairs. The white door glowed at the bottom of the stairway. White. Like the ghostly hand in Mrs. Nesbit's story. Elizabeth went down two steps. "Uncle Richard? You can stay here if you want." His footsteps were faint now. And far away.

Elizabeth hurried back up the stairs and opened her notebook. No use acting like a baby. She could look around an attic without a grown-up holding her hand. She peeked under the lids of three white boxes marked *Florida Oranges*. Each was stuffed with old garden magazines. The other boxes were sealed with tape, each with the same dull label. *Richard's work papers*. Elizabeth tapped her green pen on the empty page. No trunks. No chests. No dusty old furniture. And . . . She turned a slow circle, peering into every shadowy corner. No Jonathan.

"Okay, Jon. Where are you? You better not be playing some stupid game!" Elizabeth stood next to a stout brick chimney rising up through the floor. She crossed her arms tightly.

"I'm in here. I found a little room with toys in it." As Elizabeth bent toward the sound of his voice, she found a low, narrow passage behind the chimney. She could see Jonathan's legs on the other side, and another small, round window.

Elizabeth crawled through the passageway. "What's the password?" Jonathan blocked the opening with his arm.

"Birdbrain." Elizabeth pushed him aside and entered the small room. Jonathan turned around, about to sit on a carton in front of a toy piano.

"Jonathan, don't sit on that! We don't know what's in there."

Jonathan bent over the box. "Hey! It's marked *Grandma's Desk*."

Elizabeth knelt down. "This is the box Aunt Doris told us about! Where she thinks there might be a clue."

She lifted the cover and took out a handful of papers. One by one they studied the typewritten pages, neatly filled with dates and names like *Obediah* and *Algernon*. The names were stiff and unfamiliar, like unsmiling people in old photographs. "Gosh, I can't believe we're related to all these people."

"Here. This stuff is better." Jonathan pulled out a spotty brown envelope with a red two-cent stamp. Slowly they sifted through crinkled photos, old-fashioned Christmas cards, and handwritten notes in spidery-fine writing. Nothing even hinted of a mystery.

"Dinosaur footprints!" Jonathan sat hunched over a yellowed scrap of newspaper.

"What?"

"They found dinosaur footprints in some rocks right near the ranch in Oklahoma. It says so right here. *Tyrannosaurus rex!*" Jonathan scooped up the article and crawled through the passage. "I have to show Mom and Dad!"

"Jonathan! Forget about dinosaur footprints! We're not even done yet." Elizabeth was talking to herself now. Jonathan was already pounding down the attic stairs. She peered into the box. One cream-colored card remained on the bottom. *Thursday, September 9th, 1875,* it read. *Richmond, Ohio.* It was Grandma Lydia's wedding invitation. Elizabeth slouched against the wall with the card in her hand. Their investigation was over now. They would be leaving without a single

new clue. What was stolen? Who was P.R.? And what was Grandma Lydia trying to say about *the thirteenth*? The thirteenth what?

Elizabeth took off her glasses and pushed a damp curl out of her eye. The tiny room was as hot as a thousand summers. She wanted to get out now, back to the big and breezy kitchen. Elizabeth packed the box quickly, layer by layer. It was filled with little pieces of a life lived long ago. But not the piece they needed.

Jonathan and the others were huddled around the kitchen table discussing *Tyrannosaurus rex*. Elizabeth stood in the doorway. Maybe Elmwood House didn't have any secrets. Just an old ghost story about a creaking stair.

Elizabeth took a step into the kitchen, then stopped. A thought came to her, suddenly, like a wave hitting from behind. Without a word, she slipped into the dining room. She left her red notebook on the long, dark table, then tiptoed into the front hall. Before her, the wooden stairway curved gracefully to the second floor. Elizabeth walked up the stairs, keeping time with the slow ticking of the grandfather clock. *One, two, three.* She counted the stairs as she went up. She was just past the middle of the staircase now. *Ten, eleven, twelve.* A long, high-pitched creak answered the pressure of her next footstep. Elizabeth's hand tightened around the banister. She was right. The creaking stair was the thirteenth stair from the bottom.

"Hey, Elizabeth, what are you doing?" Jonathan skipped into the hallway, stopping at the foot of the stairway.

"I'm . . . I'm looking at the creaking stair. Jon, this is so creepy! It's the thirteenth stair from the bottom. Maybe that's what Grandma Lydia was trying to say before she died. The thirteenth *stair.*"

Jonathan walked up and stood next to Elizabeth. She pointed to the front of the stair. "And look, it's cracked. Maybe that's why it—"

Suddenly Jonathan let out a cry. For one terrible second, he teetered on the edge of the stair, about to fall backwards.

Before Elizabeth could reach out, Jonathan grabbed one of the posts supporting the banister. As he pulled on the post, it gave a sharp quarter turn to the left. This was followed by a click, then a popping sound.

Elizabeth whirled around, let out half a scream, then snapped her mouth shut. Slowly she bent toward the creaking stair. A section of wood at the front had dropped open. And behind the dark opening was a secret hiding place inside the stair.

A Secret Revealed

"What happened? Jon, are you all right?" Mr. Pollack and the other adults stood clustered at the bottom of the staircase.

"I'm okay, Dad. But I almost fell down the stairs."

"You're not going to believe what just happened!" Elizabeth moved aside to reveal the opening under the stair.

Mrs. Pollack rushed up the stairway. "Oh, no! How did you break that?"

"Mom! We didn't break anything!" Elizabeth stared into the opening. "I don't know how it happened, but Jonathan grabbed the post so he wouldn't fall. Then all of a sudden this little door popped open. Don't you see? It's a secret hiding place!"

"And it's the thirteenth stair," said Jonathan. "Elizabeth counted."

Uncle Richard disappeared into the kitchen. He hurried back with a flashlight and a handful of rags. "Don't put your hand in there yet." He knelt down in front of the opening. "This is incredible! Just incredible. I still don't understand how you found this."

"I wanted to look at the creaking stair," said Elizabeth. "I don't know. I just had this feeling it might be the thirteenth stair. Then

Jonathan came." She showed Uncle Richard exactly how Jonathan had reached out as he fell.

Uncle Richard slid his hand down the dark post supporting the banister. He gave it a gentle twist. Nothing happened until he gave the post a hard turn with both hands. This time a click sounded. A small metal latch at the top of the opening moved down. "So this is what operates the locking mechanism. You have to turn it very hard. That's why we never discovered the hiding place."

"I did notice those cracks under the stair," said Aunt Doris. "Course in an old house like this, cracks are nothing out of the ordinary. I didn't think a thing of it."

"I bet there's money in there!" Jonathan crouched in front of the stair. "'Cause Pop told us Grandma Lydia never put her money in banks."

"Well, let's find out." Uncle Richard wrapped the rag around his hand and made two quick swipes at the cobwebs under the stair. He handed the flashlight to Jonathan. "Here you go, Jonathan. You can do the honors, since you found the hiding place."

Jonathan bent down and aimed the beam into all the corners. The space inside was about twice the size of a shoe box. "I don't see anything." He groped around in the thick grey dust at the bottom. "No, wait! I can feel something!" Jonathan pulled his hand out and blew a cloud of dust into the air. "Not money. It's a letter or something."

Slowly, he unfolded a stiff sheet of paper and handed it to Uncle Richard. Both sides were covered with handwriting in faded brown ink.

Uncle Richard sat down on the stairs and patted his empty shirt pocket. "Darn it! No glasses." He held the paper at arm's length. "September 1875. And it's signed by Grandma Lydia."

"Signed by Grandma Lydia?" Elizabeth's heart was pounding like a cattle stampede. "In 1875? That's when she got married. I just found the wedding invitation in the attic."

Uncle Richard handed the paper to Mrs. Pollack. "Here—why

don't you give it a try? This needs younger eyes than mine."

Mrs. Pollack led the group into the sitting room. She sat in a narrow rocking chair next to the window, silently reading the paper. Elizabeth and Jonathan sat on the floor in front of the couch.

"Mom, come on." Elizabeth couldn't keep her knees from jiggling. "What does it say?"

"It says something about . . . P. R." Mrs. Pollack held the paper in a bright beam of sunshine and began to read aloud.

"*With heavy heart I set pen to paper this 30th day of September, 1875. I wish to make a record of the unhappy events which preceded my wedding. Once this account has been written, I shall consider the matter closed forever.*

"*September 8th, the night before my wedding, was a hot and stifling night. Thick black clouds foretold the coming of a storm. Just before midnight, not long after my parents had bid me good night, we were awakened by a servant in much distress. The treasured wedding gift which my parents had presented to me was gone! Stolen! But worse news followed. My brother Jared, while giving chase to the thief, had taken a terrible fall in the darkness. A doctor was summoned to set poor Jared's broken leg, and we comforted him as best we could. The wedding was held as planned, but it was a happy day for no one.*"

Elizabeth jumped up and put her hand on her mother's arm. "The wedding gift! It was Lydia's wedding gift from her parents that was stolen! No wonder she called it a *terrible night*. First her gift gets stolen, and then her brother breaks his leg."

Elizabeth looked at her father. "See, Dad, the note in the portrait *does* have to do with a theft. Just like I said."

Mr. Pollack threw up his hands. "Okay, I'm convinced. One hundred percent."

"Well, I want to know if they caught the thief," said Jonathan.

Mrs. Pollack turned the page over. "*Jared recognized the thief at once. It was P. R., a man who is well known to me. Just last year P. R. had begged me to marry him, and was angry when I refused. Now he has had his revenge.*

"*P. R. has not denied the theft. He simply declares over and over again that he will never reveal where the gift is hidden. And I well believe him, for never have I seen such a fierce and determined look.*

"*Yet I will not have this poor soul arrested for his crime. No jail will make him reveal the hiding place. P. R. is a strange, but not an evil, man. He fought well and bravely in the terrible battle at Shiloh. But he came back from the war a changed man, tormented by terrible nightmares and fits of rage and fear. His mind was never right again.*"

Mrs. Pollack lowered the letter into her lap. "Do you two understand what's going on?"

"Well, kind of." Elizabeth picked up the letter. "Someone with the initials *P. R.* wanted to marry Lydia, but she wouldn't. So he got back at her by taking the gift her parents gave her. I don't get the part about the battle though. Seems like Grandma Lydia felt sorry for him. She didn't want him arrested, and she didn't even use his name in the letter."

"P. R. must have been a soldier in the Civil War," said Mrs. Pollack. "I've read about the Battle of Shiloh. It was one of the bloodiest battles—thousands of soldiers were killed on both sides. From what Grandma Lydia wrote, it sounds like P. R.'s mind was never right after he came home. You know, in every war there are some soldiers who just can't stand the awful things they've seen. They're not normal for a while. Some never get back to normal."

"So Grandma Lydia felt sorry for him because of what happened in the war?" Jonathan was still sitting on the floor. He hadn't moved an inch since his mother started reading.

"And there was no point in putting the man in jail," said Mr. Pollack. "It sounds as if nothing would make him tell about the hiding place."

"Here, Mom. There's a little bit more." Elizabeth handed the letter to her mother, who continued reading aloud.

"*P. R.'s mother is greatly distressed by the terrible events. She has always treated me kindly. She gave us a handsome tea set as a wedding present. She has begged her son to return the stolen gift, but to no avail. We have been allowed to search their house and all their property. For three weeks we have searched for the gift, but our efforts have come to nothing.*

"The gift is well and cleverly hidden. It will remain lost to us; of this I am certain. Yet surely we have much to be thankful for. My brother's leg is mending nicely, and Thomas and I are well settled at the Diamond Prairie Farm. And so the time has come to forget this crime which hangs over us like a cloud. From this day on, we shall speak of the matter no more. We shall make no further efforts to find the stolen gift. But if by chance or by effort it should ever be found, I pray that it brings happiness to match the pain it has caused.

"Written on the 30th day of September, 1875

by Lydia Bailey Emerson"

Silently, Mrs. Pollack handed the letter to Uncle Richard. He folded the stiff paper and laid the letter across his hands. "I understand now. I mean, why my grandmother never spoke about this. She knew she would never find the gift, so she just tried to put it out of her mind."

"Then later," said Elizabeth, "someone sent Grandma Lydia the note about the clue in the— Wait a minute! The Blue Willow teacups! That's what the letter was talking about. They were a wedding gift from P. R.'s mother. Except Grandma Lydia never figured out the clue in the cups. So . . ."

Aunt Doris leaned forward, her round face smiling and pink. "So that means the gift could still be in its hiding place. Waiting for two young detectives to find it."

"Treasure!" Jonathan bubbled over like a can of warm soda pop. His quick footsteps were followed by the sound of the screen door slamming.

"Must be the Outer Mongolian warrior dance," said Elizabeth. "I'll go check."

She found Jonathan racing around an elm tree in the small front yard. He clutched a long, fat stick. "Treasure! Oh, yeah! We're looking for treasure!"

"Jonathan! You don't have to tell the whole world!" Elizabeth could see a face hovering behind the window blinds in the house next door.

At first Elizabeth didn't notice the man standing next to her. Then she saw the shiny white shoes. She looked up to see a man with a light blue suit and a smooth, tan face.

"Your grandpa home?" He took a toothpick out of his mouth and tossed it into the bushes. "I'm looking for Mr. Emerson. Mr. . ." He glanced inside a large black briefcase. "Mr. Richard Emerson."

"He's in the house. And he's not my grandfather." Elizabeth stared as the man climbed up the porch steps and rang the bell. There was something familiar. Something . . . Cologne. She could smell it even after he walked away. That was it. The very same cologne she had noticed in the kitchen at Diamond Prairie Farm.

Elizabeth dragged Jonathan onto the porch after the man stepped inside. "That guy was snooping around the house at Diamond Prairie."

"Yeah? How do you know?"

"Don't you remember when I . . .? Oh, never mind. Just listen." Elizabeth crouched under the porch window facing the sitting room. She could hear polite voices, then Uncle Richard's, louder. "I inherited that land from my grandmother." His voice began to sound a little like Pop's. "I'm not interested in selling it. And I know what you're up to."

Elizabeth swallowed hard. Her tongue felt as dry as a brick. Trying to buy Grandma Lydia's land. Snooping around Diamond Prairie Farm. What if the man knew about their mystery and was after the stolen wedding gift?

Suddenly the screen door squeaked open. Elizabeth and Jonathan ducked behind a wide wicker chair. They sprang out as soon as the man's sleek, white car was out of sight. Elizabeth grabbed Uncle Richard's arm as he stood on the porch.

"That man! He was at Diamond Prairie Farm. When I was in the house I could smell that yucky cologne." Elizabeth looked up the street. The white car turned at the stoplight and disappeared. "What if . . . what if he knows about Grandma Lydia's wedding gift? And he's trying to find our treasure?"

"He *is* after treasure. But not the kind you're thinking of." Uncle Richard sat down on the top step of the porch. The sunlight seemed to deepen the wrinkles in his pale face. "His name is Mr. Applegate, and he has big plans for our little farm town. You see, he's trying to buy up land. Lots of land. Then he starts building. The farms turn into houses and shopping centers." Uncle Richard stood up and gave his beard an angry tug. "This is some of the best farmland in the country. You don't just cover it over with streets and parking lots. It's too . . ." He swatted the air, as if he were shooing away a fly. "Anyway, no use going on about it. You let us worry about Mr. Applegate. You two just try and solve this mystery."

Elizabeth followed Jonathan into the house. She didn't like Mr. Applegate's plan one bit. Everything would change. The old places would be torn down and paved over. They might never find where the gift was hidden.

An hour later, as Elizabeth zipped up her suitcase, she heard Aunt Doris's heavy footsteps coming up the stairs.

"For you and Jonathan." Aunt Doris held out a small white box neatly tied with brown twine. "I packed up Grandma Lydia's teacup for you. You see, Richard and I want you to have it. This way, you'll have both cups when you find the second one."

Elizabeth held the box on her lap as they pulled away from Elmwood House. *Two matching teacups together tell the tale.* They had one cup. One half of a secret. No living person could tell them where the wedding gift was hidden. They *had* to find the second cup! And soon.

Elizabeth looked out at the hot, green land, stretching flat into forever. Suddenly the world seemed very large. And the missing teacup very, very small.

A New Lead

By early evening Jonathan and Elizabeth sat coiled like springs, ready to pop out of the car. Elizabeth pressed her face against the window as they crossed the Wabash River. The streets were narrow in the center of town, with bulky brick houses crowded shoulder to shoulder. She knew every tree, every crack in the sidewalk. Finally. They were home.

"Time to start dancing around the birdbath, Jon."

"I can't. I have to see if my sunflower grew." Jonathan scrambled out of the car and stood gaping into the backyard. Their neat garden had grown and stretched into a fairy-tale tangle of flowers. Elizabeth's tomatoes peeked out with fat, red faces. Jonathan's sunflower towered halfway to the sky.

"Mom, the butterfly garden! It worked!" Jonathan pointed to a thick hedge of orange sunflowers. A swirl of butterflies danced from flower to flower, hanging on the petals like jewels. Elizabeth smiled up at the bright yellow curtains in her bedroom window. It felt good to be home.

"I wouldn't unpack your suitcase yet." Mrs. Pollack stood in the doorway of Elizabeth's room just after dinner. "What would you think about a train trip? Dad has to stay here for some meetings, but I could spare a day or two. We could visit Pop. And Aunt Marie would be there too."

"A train trip? But, Mom, we just got back from a big trip. And tomorrow we pick up Fritzi. I don't think . . ." Elizabeth jumped up. "It's about the mystery, isn't it? You talked to Pop and he knows where the other teacup is."

Mrs. Pollack motioned her down the stairs. "Better get Jonathan. We've got some plans to make."

The decision was unanimous. At exactly 8:35 the next morning, the plans turned into action. Elizabeth followed Mrs. Pollack and Jonathan up the steep metal steps of an Amtrak train heading north.

She waved to her father as the train glided forward. Jonathan was already in a window seat, settled in with *The Encyclopedia of the Totally Disgusting*. Elizabeth glanced at the open page. "*Fun Facts About Tapeworms and Other Parasites.*"

"Uh, Mom, you know, it's very important for mothers to spend time with their sons. So I'll let you sit next to Jonathan." Elizabeth slipped into a seat across the aisle. "And then you can tell us about the box again."

"Well, I don't know very much. Pop said he has a box of odds and ends from his parents' house in Oklahoma. He doesn't remember what's in the box. It's possible—just slightly possible—that the missing teacup is in there. But first you have to find the box. He hasn't seen it in years."

Elizabeth set her red detective notebook on her lap. She didn't look at it right away. She liked to just sit and feel the sway of the train. Feel it skim over the land like a skater on a frozen pond. A train ride always seemed important, like a journey instead of just a trip. A journey to find the very last piece of the puzzle.

In Chicago they changed to a smaller train with narrow aisles and hard leather seats. At first it was full of busy-looking people with briefcases. But at the end of line, only an elderly couple and three teenagers remained. Mrs. Pollack pulled her suitcase from a high metal rack. "Aunt Marie should be here somewhere. She said she'd be driving Pop's blue car."

Fifteen minutes later, they stood alone on the platform. The train had long since pulled away. The other passengers had disappeared into waiting cars.

"How come Aunt Marie isn't here?" Jonathan dropped his backpack off his shoulder.

"I have no idea." Mrs. Pollack frowned at the drizzly sky. "But we need to find a telephone. Pop's house is still an hour away, and we can only get there by car."

She headed toward the tiny station house and pushed open a battered wooden door. A dusty window lit up two empty benches and a closed ticket window.

"Mom. There's someone here." Jonathan stepped behind his mother. A figure glided out of a shadowy corner—a blonde-haired woman, with bright red lips and two giant-sized front teeth. She held out a small bucket marked SAVE OUR DUCKS. "Buy a nut, save a duck!" She thrust forward a handful of peanuts.

Mrs. Pollack backed away. "Oh, I . . . well, you see, we were looking for a telephone."

"Telephone?" The woman set down her bucket and smiled. Her large, spotty teeth were as crooked as a train wreck. "You don't need a telephone, honey!" She bent down and placed her hand in front of her mouth. Elizabeth reached back for the door handle. The woman was . . . taking out her teeth. A moment later the blonde curls were whisked away. "Don't you recognize your sister?"

Mrs. Pollack's sister stood before them, a wig in one hand and a set of fake teeth in the other. Elizabeth took her hand off the door. "Aunt Marie! But those teeth! I mean, you're a dentist."

Aunt Marie swept all three into a hug. She was slender and dark-haired like Mrs. Pollack, but louder and quicker to laugh. Like a brighter shade of the same color. "Quite a set of choppers, aren't they? They were a big hit at the dental convention last month. You see, I won a gift certificate from Jack's Joke Shop." She patted Jonathan's shoulder. "If you're good, I'll let you use my vampire fangs."

Jonathan let out a whoop. "Know what? You're even better than *The Encyclopedia of the Totally Disgusting!*"

"Well, . . . uh, thanks." Aunt Marie laughed. "I just like to spice things up a bit. I mean, everyone else simply got off the train and climbed into a car. But *you*, on the other hand, have had an experience."

By the time they arrived at Pop's house, the drizzle had worked itself into a downpour. Jonathan and Elizabeth raced into the house, stopping just inside the back door. With the rain pressing on the window panes, the kitchen looked smaller, more worn and tired.

"What took you so long? I expected you half an hour ago." Pop sat at the head of the kitchen table, like a judge ready to hand down a sentence. He set his cigar stump on a small ashtray. "But I'm glad you're here. Get those wet shoes off and come over here. I have something to show you two detectives."

Elizabeth stepped forward, pulling Jonathan along by his shirt sleeve. She could see her mother and Aunt Marie still waiting in the car.

"Your mother told me about your discoveries." Pop tapped his forehead. "Glad to hear you know how to use your heads. Course your old grandpappy's not such a bad detective either." Pop straightened up and puffed out his chest. "This man P. R. The one who stole my grandmother's wedding gift. I've discovered his last name. It's Rutledge."

"But how could you do that?" Jonathan took a step closer.

Pop held up a frayed sheet of paper. "I found this in a carton of old papers. It's my grandmother Lydia's list of wedding gifts. We know that P. R.'s mother gave a tea set as a wedding present. She's listed right here." Elizabeth took the paper. She recognized Grandma Lydia's graceful handwriting. "*Mrs. Marion Rutledge—Blue Willow tea set.*"

"Good job, Pop." Jonathan gave his grandfather a cautious pat on the back.

"And I bet we could find out his first name," said Elizabeth. "I learned about it in social studies. You can use old records to find out about people who lived a long time ago. Maybe Uncle Richard could do that for us."

"I've already called my brother and given him the name. He's going to look at the county records first thing tomorrow morning."

Jonathan stuck his head into a narrow broom closet next to the refrigerator. "So now can we start looking for that box? The one where the teacup might be."

"All right," said Pop. "Now pay attention. You're looking for a cardboard box a little bigger than a shoe box. And it's marked *Antlers, Oklahoma*. That's where my parents lived after they sold the ranch."

Elizabeth thought about her detective manual. *Chapter Four— Searching for Lost Items.* "When was the last time you saw the box, Pop?"

"Oh, I haven't seen it in years. Not since the quilt room was painted. Look upstairs in all the closets and underneath the beds. I don't know where else it could be."

Jonathan and Elizabeth headed into the living room. Their mother and Aunt Marie stomped through the back door. Pop's voice followed. "Just don't break anything!"

"We know," called Jonathan. "And keep the bedroom door closed. Do *not* let Cat into the room."

"Don't worry. She's down here." Elizabeth saw a bulky shadow dart under the black leather couch. She stood for a moment and glanced up at the portrait. Joshua Bailey stared straight ahead, as stern and somber as the rain.

"How come you're always staring at stuff?" Jonathan stopped, halfway up the stairs.

"Because I like to think. You can't be a detective without thinking."

"Well, I don't have to think. I'm gonna go look in the quilt room. In the closet." Elizabeth heard a door creak open, then bang shut. Jonathan stumbled back down the stairs. "The box isn't in there."

"Jonathan, you were only gone for two seconds. You didn't even look."

"I . . . I saw a shrunken head. Hanging on a hook."

"Yeah, right. I'm sure Pop keeps shrunken heads in all the closets. And anyway, I thought you liked stuff like that."

Elizabeth marched into the small room at the top of the stairs. Jonathan sat on the edge of the bed, picking nervously at the old patchwork quilt. "You'll see. It's all wrinkled and hairy. And it has teeth. I bet Pop got it on one of his trips."

Elizabeth slowly opened the closet door. She shined her flashlight into the long, narrow space. "Relax, Tarzan. It's just a coconut head." She held up a coconut with carved eyes and white seeds that looked like teeth. "Now quit being such a baby. We have to get to work."

Jonathan followed Elizabeth from room to room. They peered under all the beds and dug around in deep dresser drawers. Jonathan was sent into the very back of each closet.

"Find anything?" Elizabeth held the flashlight as Jonathan crawled into Pop's closet.

"Nope. Just Christmas ornaments. And a cigar box full of pictures." He handed the box out to Elizabeth.

"That's it. The last closet." Elizabeth clicked off her flashlight. "Anyway, Pop's yelling. So dinner must be ready."

"I don't eat raw string beans!" Pop stood over the stove, jabbing his fork into a pot. "Cook 'em till they're mush. That's what I say."

"This is all we found, Pop." Elizabeth handed him the cigar box full of old photographs. Jonathan held up a fake arm he found sticking out of Aunt Marie's suitcase.

Pop ignored the fake arm. "Now, look. The box is marked ANT-LERS, OKLAHOMA, and it's somewhere in this house. I thought you two were ace detectives."

"But . . ." Elizabeth shook her head. "We have to leave tomorrow. And we've already looked everywhere."

Aunt Marie shooed Pop away from the stove. "Tell you what.

Your mom and I have to help Pop with something after breakfast. But after that we'll have time to help you. I'm sure we'll find it." She took the fake arm and patted Jonathan's shoulder with the soft plastic hand. "And you can take this home with you. My compliments."

After dinner, Pop sat between Elizabeth and Jonathan on the black leather couch. He set the box of photographs on his knee.

"Take a look at this one." He pulled out a small black and white snapshot. "It's a picture of me with Grandma Lydia. We were in front of the Diamond Prairie Farm."

Elizabeth leaned over. "We went there! Jonathan and I even searched the house." She laid the photo in the palm of her hand. Pop was slim and dark-haired. He had his arm around a tiny woman in a prim black hat. Behind them were two pillars, each with a diamond-shaped stone set into it.

Elizabeth gazed at Grandma Lydia, who looked small and frail.

She tried to picture the young bride whose wedding gift was stolen.

"Look, Pop, this is Button, isn't it?" Jonathan fished out a picture of a man sitting straight and serious on a light-colored horse.

"You're right. This is my father on his favorite horse." Pop squinted his eyes at Elizabeth. She hoped he wasn't going to complain about her hair again. "Maybe you two should become the official family historians."

Elizabeth looked at Jonathan. "Well, I guess we could."

"*Guess?* What you mean *guess?*" Pop's voice turned cranky. "Either you want to or you don't."

"I mean, sure, Jon and I could be the family historians. And I was thinking . . . Well, I like to write. I could write down some of your stories from the ranch. Or maybe put you on a videotape."

The word *video* set Pop off like a firecracker. "Machines. Kids are addicted to machines, I tell you. Television. Computer. Video games. That's all they—wait a minute! What did you say?"

"I said I could write down some of your stories about the ranch. Or I could make a tape." Pop leaned back with a grunt of approval.

"I thought you were going to write about me!" said Jonathan. "About all the bad stuff I do."

"Don't worry, Jon. I have enough material on you for a two-volume set."

"And I can give you lots more stuff to— Oh, wow!" Jonathan's eyes widened. Pop's head was tilted back, his mouth open wide as a train tunnel. He made an unearthly sound, something between a long moan and a tornado siren.

"Gosh, Pop. I wish I could yawn like that. Maybe we can get it on tape."

Elizabeth thought about Pop before she went to sleep that night. She was sure none of her friends had grandfathers like him. Her mother said he was the kind of person who made life interesting.

Elizabeth stretched over to the night table and snapped off the light. Only one thing would make *her* life interesting. Finding the box and the second teacup.

She slid her toes to the end of the bed. The sheets felt cool and . . . fingers? She was out of bed in an instant, whipping back the covers.

"Very funny!"

She grabbed the fake arm and slipped into the hallway. She eased open Jonathan's door, careful not to wake him. Then gently, very gently, she placed the arm next to Jonathan's cheek. *Life with Brother.* Volume three.

Cat Turns Detective

Early the next morning, Elizabeth and Jonathan found Pop banging around in the kitchen. Elizabeth wished the day didn't seem so ordinary. Cereal boxes on the counter. The dull hum of a fishing boat on the lake. This day had to be special. Otherwise their mystery would be over. Just a good story without an ending.

Mrs. Pollack and Aunt Marie shuffled to the table in their robes and slippers. Aunt Marie set down her coffee cup.

"You know, I've been thinking about your mystery. You kids have done a great job, but there's one thing that puzzles me. What was the wedding gift that was stolen?"

"We don't know," said Elizabeth. "Grandma Lydia just said it was a gift from her parents."

"I've got it!" Pop's fist thundered down on the table. Jonathan dropped his spoon, and Elizabeth wiped a wet corn flake off her cheek.

"Bring me that piece of paper." Pop grabbed Jonathan by the shoulder. "The one with the wedding gifts."

Elizabeth already knew why Pop was so excited. "I can't believe we've been so stupid! We looked at the list of wedding gifts last night. The gift from Lydia's parents must be written on there too."

Everyone clustered around Pop's chair. Pop frowned as he pointed to a thick black line. The very first entry had been crossed out. Elizabeth held the paper up against the window. The words were gone forever, hidden under a dark streak of ink.

"Too bad," said Mrs. Pollack. "I guess Grandma Lydia didn't even want to see the gift on her wedding list."

Elizabeth sat down hard and stared into her corn flakes. "This case is going to drive me crazy. Everything happened so long ago. And people are always hiding clues and crossing things out."

Pop waved a hand in the direction of the living room. "Telephone's ringing."

"I'll go." Aunt Marie hurried out of the kitchen. She came back a few minutes later holding a piece of paper.

"That was Uncle Richard. And he had some news. He found out that Marion Rutledge had two children, a daughter and a son." Aunt Marie looked down at the paper. "The son's name was Peter. Peter Rutledge. He was a soldier in the Civil War. He came back to Ohio after the war and lived until 1890."

"So that's our mysterious P. R.," said Mrs. Pollack. "Peter Rutledge. Seems like everything is falling into place."

"Yeah, everything except the teacup." Elizabeth grabbed Jonathan's bowl before he could think about a second helping. "Come on. Let's start looking again."

Jonathan raced into the living room ahead of Elizabeth. "I'm going to get the detective notebook. So you can write down that guy's name. Peter Rutledge."

"You better stay out of my backpack, Jonathan. That's my stuff."

"Hey, I bet your diary's in here." Jonathan grabbed the backpack off the couch. He scrambled up the stairs like a runaway chimp.

Elizabeth reached the quilt room just in time to have the door slammed in her face. "Give it here, Jonathan." She could feel

Jonathan's weight against the door. When she leaned in with her shoulder, the door gave way. Jonathan stumbled backwards into the bookcase. Pop's globe wobbled, then crashed to the floor.

"Jonathan, you are such an idiot." Hard, quick footsteps pounded up the stairs. "And now Mom is coming."

Jonathan stuck out his tongue. "Idiot yourself."

Mrs. Pollack stood in the doorway. Jonathan dove to the floor, faking a painful collapse.

"Well, I guess you think fighting is more important than looking for the box. And don't start blaming each other. I don't care who started it. You two need to be separated for a while." She looked down at Jonathan. "You stay in here. Elizabeth, you go in the other bedroom. I'll tell you when you can come out."

Elizabeth grabbed her backpack and flopped onto the bed in the next room. She ripped a sheet of paper from her journal. *Ode to Jonathan.* She scribbled the words with a dull pencil. *How annoying are you? Let me count the ways. 1. idiotic, 2. irritating, 3. impossible.* Elizabeth put her pencil down after number 12. *buzzard-brained.* She wasn't so mad anymore. And anyway, she was running out of adjectives.

She turned to the wall above her bed and knocked five times. It was their code for *Do you want to talk?* Jonathan knocked once in reply. *Yes.* Seven knocks from Elizabeth. *Open your door.* One knock in reply. *Yes.*

Elizabeth peered into the hallway. Jonathan's door was still closed. As it slowly swung open, the fake hand slid out and clawed the carpet.

"Jonathan, quit fooling around. We've got to start looking for the box."

Jonathan laid the arm on the floor. The two stretched out in the narrow hallway, keeping their feet in separate rooms. "We're not mad any more," Jonathan shouted down the stairs. "Can we come out?"

Their mother's voice came from the kitchen. "All right. But no more fighting."

"I don't get what we're supposed to do." Jonathan sat in the middle of the hallway. "We've already looked everywhere."

"My detective manual . . ." Elizabeth grabbed Jonathan's arm to prevent escape. "My detective manual says you have to look in the most likely places a second time. Because it's easy to miss something. For one thing, we didn't really search the high shelves of the closets very well."

Elizabeth dragged a wooden chair from closet to closet. She discovered a lime green golf umbrella and a musty snowsuit. When Mrs. Pollack and Aunt Marie joined the search, Pop supervised from downstairs. "Look under the beds! And keep Cat out of the bedrooms!"

For the next hour the house was searched again, top to bottom. Nothing. Finally, Elizabeth gave up. She slumped into a padded rocking chair by the picture window. Jonathan fiddled with the fireplace tongs.

"I'm afraid it's time to start packing." Mrs. Pollack glanced up at the fortune-teller clock, still softly ticking on the mantel. "We can't miss our train." Elizabeth and Jonathan stared at the floor. "Sorry, kids. But I start teaching next week. I have a lot of work to do."

Aunt Marie stretched out on the floor and peered under the black couch. "Don't worry. We know the box is here somewhere. I usually stop by once a week or so. I'll keep looking."

Elizabeth blinked hard, trying to make her eyes stop feeling watery. "Sure, Aunt Marie. Thanks." She and Jonathan shuffled up the stairs and closed their backpacks. The fake arm was still on the floor next to Jonathan's bed. "Don't forget your fake arm, Jon. You might want to put it in my bed again."

Jonathan reached down, then drew his hand back quickly. The fake arm was . . . moving. Slowly, the fingers slid under the bed and disappeared behind the quilt.

Elizabeth bent down. "Just what we need! The cat's under here again. How come she does this every time we have to leave?"

"What are you doing up there?" Pop's voice rang out right on cue.

"We're almost ready." Jonathan knelt down and made a grab. The cat disappeared behind the folding chairs stored under the bed.

"Jon, why did you do that? We'll never get her out now."

Jonathan crawled around to the foot of the bed and turned on his flashlight. "Okay. I can see her. Hey, wait! There's something else under there. It looks like a box! It's way back behind the chairs."

"A box?" Elizabeth dropped to her knees. "Quick. Let's get the cat out. Then we can . . . Jonathan?" Jonathan disappeared into the closet. He came out carrying the coconut head.

"Abandon ship!" He thrust it under the bed and let out a howl. A perfect imitation of Pop's yawn. The cat bounded out the door and down the stairs.

"I've got the box." Jonathan's red stocking feet stuck out from under the bed. Elizabeth pulled him out by the ankles. He came out dragging a grey metal box.

"But, Jon, that's not it! Pop said it's cardboard."

Jonathan sat with the box in his lap. "I don't care. The box says ANTLERS, OKLAHOMA, just like Pop said." Jonathan pushed at the lid. "But I can't open it."

Elizabeth looked at a keyhole at the front of the box. "The key! Remember we found that little key in the old dresser." She jumped up and tugged open the heavy top drawer.

The small metal key slid in easily. Elizabeth flipped open the top. "Papers again. Just boring . . ." But as she lifted a handful of letters, she spotted a curved handle and . . . Elizabeth held her breath . . . a very tiny, very blue Chinese pagoda.

Jonathan scooped up the cup. "This is it! Just like the other one!"

"We found it!" Elizabeth shouted. She cradled the cup in her hands as she raced into the kitchen. Jonathan did two laps around the table as he told the story. The cat. The folding chairs under the bed. The key from the old dresser. Pop dropped his cigar and had to slap the ashes off his pants.

They had no time to celebrate. Aunt Marie wrapped the cup in newspaper and gave it to Elizabeth in a small cloth bag. Jonathan

stuffed the fake arm into Mrs. Pollack's backpack. "Sorry, Mom. I don't have room for it."

"Well, you can carry this." Pop handed Jonathan the cigar box full of photos. "If you're going to be the family historians, you can start by sorting out these pictures."

Pop gave Elizabeth and Jonathan stiff pats on the shoulder as they climbed into Aunt Marie's car. "I like it when you come, you know. It gets . . ." Pop's grumble died down to a slow, shaky whisper. "It gets lonely here."

Pop started toward the house, then turned around with his arms in the air. "Slow down!" His voice sent two squirrels scurrying up a tree. "Don't hit that garbage can!" Elizabeth smiled. Pop was his old self again.

"We're just in time." Aunt Marie kissed them good-bye on the platform. "You kids go ahead. I just need to fix your mother's backpack." Jonathan and Elizabeth hoisted themselves onto the train. They walked past a lively group of women speaking a language Elizabeth couldn't understand. "They're from Russia," whispered Jonathan. "I heard the conductor say so."

"We're back here, Mom!" Elizabeth waved at her mother. As Mrs. Pollack made her way down the aisle, the other passengers stopped talking, one by one. By the time Mrs. Pollack reached her seat, the car was quiet as a church. Twenty pair of eyes stared at her.

"Uh . . . Mom. I think Aunt Marie was spicing things up again." Elizabeth saw a pinkish glow spread over her mother's face. "Better take a look at your backpack. She fixed it so the hand is sticking out."

The pink ripened to a deep red. Mrs. Pollack pulled out the fake arm and dangled it in front of her. "Joke." She spoke slowly, dragging out the long *o*. "Joke." The Russian ladies stared, still looking alarmed. Finally, a curly haired young woman smiled and nodded her head. "Joke! Okay. You make good joke." She turned and spoke to the others in Russian. A short lady in a green pants suit stood up and clapped.

"Gosh, Mom, you're lucky." Jonathan reached out for the fake arm. "Everybody else just got on the train and found a seat. But *you* have had an experience."

Elizabeth zipped open her backpack, then closed it again. She couldn't do puzzles. She couldn't read. She couldn't even look out the window. All she could do was stare at the white cloth bag. Grandma Lydia's wedding gift was stolen in 1875. And now they had the two Blue Willow teacups that would tell them where to find it.

Will the Tale Be Told?

"Dad! We found the teacup!" The train doors were still closed. Jonathan bobbed up and down behind a wide women with a large suitcase.

"You what?" Mr. Pollack stepped closer as the wide metal door opened.

"We have the teacup." Elizabeth held up the white cloth bag as she climbed down the steps. By the time the train pulled out of the station Jonathan had shouted out the whole story.

"And lots of other stuff happened too. Aunt Marie gave me a fake arm and Mom was carrying it in her backpack. And Aunt Marie fixed it so the hand was sticking out, only Mom didn't know it, and there were these Russian people on the train, and they were looking kind of worried. So Mom's face got all red, and she told them it was only a joke. Except they didn't understand at first. And when they did, they clapped. Oh, and I almost forgot. Aunt Marie has some yucky fake teeth. And I want some too."

Mr. Pollack gave a half smile. "Sounds like a typical weekend with Marie." He opened the car door. "And by the way, I picked up a friend of yours. He's waiting for you at home."

Elizabeth didn't have to ask—their parakeet Fritzi was back. They hadn't seen him since they left for Maine.

"Hey, Fritzi, we're back!" Elizabeth raced into her bedroom just ahead of Jonathan. Fritzi rang his bell and puffed up his feathers. "*Call the police. Under arrest.*"

"We can't go to jail right now, Fritzi. We've got work to do."

Elizabeth ran down to the kitchen. She set the teacups on the round wooden table. "So what's the clue?" Jonathan skidded into a chair next to her.

"It won't just pop out at us, Jon. I mean, if the clue was really easy, Grandma Lydia would have figured it out a hundred years ago." Elizabeth picked up the cups, one by one. The pictures didn't look very real. The trees were round and puffy, like piles of cotton balls. The birds were almost as big as the houses. And they faced each other in the air, as if one were flying backwards.

"Looks like two regular old teacups to me." Jonathan began tapping his foot, then bouncing an imaginary ball. "Uh . . . I'll be right back." Elizabeth could hear the basketball bouncing on the driveway.

She cranked open the kitchen window. "Jonathan, you can't just give up right way. Mom's going to make us go to bed pretty soon and . . . Oh, never mind." Elizabeth gathered up the cups and put them into a high cabinet in the dining room. They could try again tomorrow. She would call her friend Becky, then look at *How To Think Like a Detective*. Fresh ideas. That's what she needed.

The next morning, Elizabeth sat on the floor of her room. She tightened her ponytail and wiped her glasses on her Chicago Cubs T-shirt. "The meeting of the Pollack Detective Agency will now come to order." She set the Blue Willow teacups, side by side, on the rose-colored carpet. When Jonathan came in, Fritzi sailed down from the curtain rod and landed on his shoulder.

"*'Scuse me. Did you brush you teeth?*" Fritzi lifted his head and puffed out his neck. "*'Scuse me, 'scuse me—Idiot!*"

"Yes, Fritzi. We've both brushed our teeth. Okay, Jonathan." Elizabeth got up and closed the door firmly. "We're going to do something called brainstorming."

Jonathan sank to the floor. "I know. There's a whole chapter about it in your detective manual."

"Exactly. You're learning, Jonathan." Elizabeth sat down between Jonathan and the door. "All right. Brainstorming means we say any idea we think of, no matter what it is. Everything gets written down. Then later we see which ideas are best."

Jonathan looked at the door with a sigh. "Well, I can think of one thing. The teacups might have a hidden clue. And maybe you have to use a magnifying glass to see it. Like Abraham Lincoln on the back of a penny. If you don't have a magnifying glass, you can hardly see him."

"Good idea. I'll put that on the list." Elizabeth opened the red notebook and shooed Fritzi away as he nibbled her pen.

"How's the investigation coming?" Mr. Pollack walked into the room a half hour later.

"Pretty good," said Elizabeth. "We came up with five ideas." She looked at her notes. "One, look at the cups through a magnifying glass. Two, hold the cups up to the light to look for secret writing. Three, get information about the Blue Willow pattern. Four, find out if Uncle Richard knows about any bridge that looks like the one on the cups. And five, see if the cups are different in any way."

Elizabeth closed her notebook. "But we're not getting too far. We couldn't find any secret writing. And we looked at all the pictures and those little triangles at the top. The two cups are just the same."

"But I found something with the magnifying glass!" Jonathan stood next to his father. "See these marks on the bridge? When you look close, you can see what they are. Three people crossing the bridge." Fritzi landed on Jonathan's hand and gave the teacup a cautious peck. "Except we still don't know what the clue is."

"Well, I can help you out with one thing." Mrs. Pollack laid a stack of folded laundry on Elizabeth's bed. "I'll call Uncle Richard tonight. See if he knows of a bridge like the one on the cup."

Elizabeth stood up and stretched. "And we'll ride our bikes to the library. Maybe they have something about the Blue Willow pattern."

Elizabeth and Jonathan burst in through the back door just before lunch. Elizabeth heaved a heavy book onto the shiny wood of the dining room table. "Mom, this is great! I think we found a new lead."

"It's about a Chinese maiden." Jonathan worked his voice into a coo. "A love story."

"Jonathan Pollack? Excited about a love story?" Mrs. Pollack put her hand on Jonathan's forehead.

"Yeah. See, we found out the pictures on the teacup tell a story."

Elizabeth opened up the book. "Look at this, Mom. There's a legend that goes with the Blue Willow pattern. See, there was this Chinese man, and he tried to make his daughter marry a rich man. She wouldn't do it, because the man was really old and she didn't even like him. And anyway, she was in love with someone else her own age. So they ran away together, and her father chased them." Elizabeth took the cups out of the high cabinet. "You can see the three of them on the bridge."

"And then comes the bad part," said Jonathan. "They escape and go live on an island. But the old man finds them. And he burns down their house because he's mad she wouldn't marry him. So the maiden and the guy she loves both get killed. And you know those two doves on the teacups? Those are supposed to be their spirits."

"So Lydia would be like the girl in the story." Mrs. Pollack picked up one of the teacups. "She wouldn't marry Peter Rutledge, and he got revenge by stealing the gift." She handed the cup to Jonathan. "Anyway, I'm glad you two made some progress. I called Uncle Richard about the bridge. There's no bridge anything like the one on the cups."

Elizabeth and Jonathan sat on the cement steps leading to the front door. Elizabeth set the book on her lap and read the story out loud three times. After the third time, she stared at the page without speaking. The legend was interesting. But what about the clue? How did the story tell them where to look for the stolen wedding gift?

By the end of the week Elizabeth was in a gloomy mood. It was Friday night, almost time for bed, and school would be starting on Monday. Everyone had studied the teacups. Her parents. Her friends. Even the man next door. No one could see anything but two ordinary teacups.

Elizabeth cleared all the puzzle books off her desk. She set the cups on the dark wood. She stared at the teacups from every direction, glared at them until her eyes burned. No wonder Grandma Lydia never found the clue. It was just too hard. Or maybe the note was some kind of joke.

Jonathan appeared in the doorway and slid a long box across the floor. Elizabeth glanced at the cover of the board game. "No way, Jonathan."

"But you promised. You broke my fishing pole when we were in Maine, and you said you'd play a game with me. Any one I want."

Elizabeth backed away from the box. *Encyclopedia of the Totally Disgusting—The Companion Board Game*. Anything but that.

"It's scientific. You find out how a piece of pizza gets digested. The board shows all your insides. We each get three markers. And they start in the saliva in the mouth, then get into the stomach acid. You can see how the pizza is all mushed up and. . ."

"Jonathan, this is disgusting."

"But you promised."

"Oh, all right. But just one game." After her third turn, Elizabeth stretched her arm back and quietly slid open Fritzi's cage door. Time for birdie bowling. After Fritzi flew onto her finger, she lowered him to the floor. Strike. He pattered across the game board and knocked down all six markers. With a red marker in his mouth, he did a fast waddle across the carpet.

Jonathan groaned. "Cut it out, Fritzi! I was almost to the large intestine."

"Oh, sorry, Jon. I don't remember where my markers were. So I declare you the winner." Elizabeth quickly packed up the game. "Now, Fritzi. Don't you do that again."

Elizabeth stood up. "But don't go, Jon. Let's just give the teacups one more try."

They sat on the floor, cups in the middle, like so many times before. Fritzi hopped up on the rim, dropping Jonathan's red marker into the teacup. Jonathan shooed him away. "Here, this will keep him out." He put one cup on top of the other so the rims were touching.

"Hey, look!" Jonathan laid on the floor with his head near the cups. "When you put the cups together like that, the triangles at the top come together."

"Jonathan, quit fooling around. You could chip the cups." Elizabeth shook her head. Some detective agency. Working with a kid brother who couldn't be serious for a minute. "Anyway, what are you talking about?"

"The triangles at the top of the cups. When they come together they make . . ." Jonathan looked at Elizabeth. "They make diamonds."

Diamonds. The word hung in the air like a brightly colored balloon.

"Diamond Prairie Farm!" They spoke the words at the same time.

"That's the clue! It has to be!" Elizabeth was on her hands and knees, staring at the cups. "When you put the cups on top of each other, the triangles come together to make diamonds. Someone was trying to tell Grandma Lydia the gift was hidden at Diamond Prairie Farm!"

Jonathan ran to the top of the stairs. "Mom! Dad! We have to tell you something!"

"What's this all about?" Mr. and Mrs. Pollack hurried up the stairs. Jonathan and Elizabeth stood in the middle of the room. Fritzi was on Jonathan's head, standing at attention.

"Me, Elizabeth, and Fritzi the wonder parakeet." Jonathan made himself tall. "We just found the clue in the teacups."

Elizabeth held up the two cups with their rims touching. "Look what happens when the two cups are together. The triangles make diamonds. Like Diamond Prairie Farm!"

"*Two matching teacups together tell the tale.*" Mrs. Pollack ran her finger along the band of diamonds. "So the cups have to be put together. Really, physically, put together to get the clue. No wonder Grandma Lydia didn't think of that."

"And we were always looking at the pictures," said Elizabeth. "We never paid attention to the triangles along the top."

Elizabeth glanced at her father. He hadn't said a word. "I know, Dad. You're looking at this like a scientist. And you think we're wrong."

"No, I think you're right. It's just that . . . well, I don't know how the clue helps us. If the stolen gift is at Diamond Prairie, it could be hidden anywhere on the farm. We still have no idea where to look."

"Wait! We do know where to look!" Elizabeth rushed into her closet. "I'll tell you one thing. It's lucky Jonathan and I decided to be family historians. The last piece of the puzzle is right here." She held up the cigar box of photographs from Pop's house.

"It is?" Jonathan peered into the box.

"Don't you remember? The picture of Pop and Grandma Lydia at the Diamond Prairie Farm. You can see what the stone pillars were like before the vines grew."

Elizabeth held up the tiny photo. Set into the stones and mortar of each pillar was a piece of limestone—a piece of limestone in the shape of a diamond.

Jonathan grabbed the magnifying glass from Elizabeth's desk. "I can read the words in the diamond. It says Diamond Prairie Farm. And there's a date too. Eighteen . . . seventy-nine."

"Eighteen-seventy-nine!" Elizabeth grinned at her father. "The same date as the note."

"Now you're on to something." Mr. Pollack ran his hand through his hair as he paced around the room. "That must be the year when the fence and the pillars were built. The ground would have been dug up. Peter Rutledge could have easily buried something there."

Elizabeth sat down on the edge of her bed. She tried to make her mind slow down, go over everything step by step. The diamonds were the clue in the teacup. A diamond was on each pillar at the Diamond Prairie Farm. Peter Rutledge stole the gift in 1875. Four years later he saw the pillars being built. The perfect new hiding place.

Jonathan gazed at the picture. "When Pop and Grandma Lydia were having their picture taken, they were standing right on top of the treasure!"

"And now the last sentence of the note makes sense," said Mr. Pollack. "*Remember this—you have it yet have it not.* Grandma Lydia *did* have the gift, but she didn't know it. The stolen wedding gift was buried right in front of her house at the Diamond Prairie Farm."

"Mom, I can't believe we . . . Where did Mom go?" Elizabeth looked into the hallway.

"I don't know. I think I heard the phone ringing," said Jonathan.

"I'm right here." Mrs. Pollack's footsteps sounded slow and hesitant on the stairs. "That was Uncle Richard on the phone."

"What did he say?" Elizabeth didn't like the look on her mother's face.

"He said . . . He said his cousin, the one who owns Diamond Prairie Farm . . . Well, she decided to sell it to Mr. Applegate. The man who wants to build houses."

"No!" Elizabeth jumped off the bed. "She can't! It's still there!" She took the photo from her father and waved it in the air. "The treasure is still there!"

Hunting for Treasure

"Mom, are you done yet? You've been on the phone all morning." Elizabeth swung open the kitchen door. She and Jonathan had been pacing and pestering and were finally banned from the kitchen. "What did Pop's cousin say about selling the house?"

Mrs. Pollack sat back in the kitchen chair and stretched out her legs. "Good news. She hasn't signed any papers yet. Now that she knows about the clue, she won't sell the property. Not now, anyway."

"And did you talk to Uncle Richard again? And Pop and Aunt Marie?" Jonathan hopped around the table.

"Well, I told all of them about the clue. But it's strange. Every one of them is sick."

"But how could they all be sick?" Elizabeth sat down next to her mother.

"Fever!" Mrs. Pollack leaped off her chair. "They've got treasure-hunting fever. Watch out, it's contagious!" She grabbed Jonathan and dragged him into a polka around the kitchen table.

Elizabeth pressed herself against the wall. "Mom, are you going crazy, or what?"

After Jonathan wriggled out of his mother's arms, the three sat around the kitchen table.

"It's all set," said Mrs. Pollack. "We leave for Ohio in two weeks. Aunt Marie will pick up Pop. We'll all meet at a motel near Uncle Richard's house. And, by the way, we have to leave on a Friday. You two will miss half a day of school." Jonathan gave Elizabeth a thumbs-up sign behind his back.

Elizabeth kept the cups, side by side, in a cubby in her white bookcase. Sometimes, just before bed, she would set one cup on top of the other. She would stare at the blue triangles, watch them make a perfect row of diamonds where they came together. The diamonds were the clue. She was sure. At least she tried to be sure. But every day she grew less certain. On the night before the trip to Ohio, she was still awake when her parents turned off the late news. She heard her mother's footsteps in the hallway.

"Mom, can you come in my room?"

"What's wrong? Too excited to sleep?"

"Not exactly excited." Elizabeth sat up in bed. "I was so happy about finding the clue, but now I keep thinking maybe we're not right. Maybe the row of diamonds isn't the right clue. Maybe nothing's buried in front of the pillar. And even if we're right, what if the gift rotted away from being buried so long? I don't know. Everybody's so excited. And I'm afraid it's going to be nothing. I almost wish we hadn't told anyone."

"There's only one way to look at it." Mrs. Pollack sat down on Elizabeth's bed. "You and Jonathan aren't just pretending. You're real detectives now. You figured out the meaning of that strange old note hidden in the portrait. And you uncovered secrets no one else knew about." She stroked a strand of hair off Elizabeth's forehead. "Don't you see what's happened? All this interest in family history. You and Jonathan have become memory keepers. Just like Pop and Uncle Richard. Nothing can change that."

"I know, Mom. But it would be terrible to solve the mystery and then not find the treasure."

Elizabeth laid her head back on the pillow. Her mother was still talking, but the words were floating now, soft and far away. Elizabeth closed her eyes for just a moment. When she opened them again, she sat up with a jolt. The morning was already bright and busy. A tea kettle whistled in the kitchen. Jonathan was outside her door, yelling something about the last two toaster waffles.

At school that morning, Elizabeth spent most of her time checking her watch. "Sorry about the holes in the paper, Mrs. Dexter. I had to do a lot of erasing." Elizabeth handed her teacher a raggedy worksheet on dividing fractions.

Mrs. Dexter picked up the paper by the corner and held it up like a dirty rag. "*Not* one of your best efforts, I would say."

At the sound of the lunch bell, Elizabeth shot out of the room. She collided with Jonathan on the stairs. They hurried home at a fast trot and ran upstairs to close their suitcases.

By the time Mr. Pollack arrived home from the high school, three suitcases were lined up in the trunk of the car. "I can't find my *Encyclopedia of the Totally Disgusting*." Jonathan stood scowling in the driveway. "I always take it on trips."

Elizabeth shrugged her shoulders and pressed her lips together so she wouldn't smile. Jonathan's favorite book had somehow found its way underneath his bed. Far underneath. Sad that he didn't know it. Elizabeth looked forward to a pleasant trip.

Mrs. Pollack closed the trunk. "Now, when we get to Ohio, don't expect anything fancy. Pop didn't want to spend too much money on a motel."

"I can see what you mean about the motel, Mom." It was almost dinner time when Elizabeth spotted a faded orange and green sign reading E-Z Rest Motor Lodge. The plastic *Z* was dangling upside down beneath the other letters. Pop's old Chevy was parked next to an empty swimming pool with peeling paint.

"I see Pop!" Elizabeth jumped out of the car and peered into a shabby motel office. "And Aunt Marie. Oh, gross! She has her fake teeth in, and she's giving a great big smile."

A straggly haired young woman stood behind the counter, chomping on a wad of gum. She held out two keys at arm's length, leaning away from Aunt Marie's dark tangle of teeth. "Rooms thirty-one and thirty-two. Check out time is eleven a.m."

Aunt Marie turned toward the door. "Oh, super! The rest of our fam-a-lee has arrived!"

"The rest . . . of your family?" The clerk jerked her head up, chewing her gum at a full gallop. Mrs. Pollack pushed open the door and put her arm around Aunt Marie.

"All right, Marie. Take those off and give this young lady some peace of mind."

The clerk leaned over the counter. A bright green wad of gum fell out of her mouth as Aunt Marie pried out her fake teeth. Jonathan stayed for a moment after the others had left. "Don't worry. She just likes to spice things up."

As soon as the cars were unpacked, they set out for Elmwood House. Eight places were set at the long, dark table in the dining room.

"I hope the treasure is something good. Like a chest full of gold." Jonathan dropped a thick slice of ham onto his plate.

Elizabeth rolled her eyes. "Jon, this is a wedding present, not a pirate treasure."

"Well, I've been thinking about the gift, too" said Uncle Richard. "You know, Joshua Bailey gave the Diamond Prairie Farm to both my grandparents. But the gift Peter Rutledge stole. I think it may have been something special just for Grandma Lydia."

"Silver!" Pop banged on the table, narrowly missing Aunt Doris's cheesy potato bake. "The Baileys were great ones for giving sterling silver. A fancy tea service. That's my guess."

"Elizabeth, you haven't told us what you think." Aunt Doris untied her apron as she sat down.

"Oh, I don't know really." Elizabeth didn't look up. The gift could be . . . nothing. They could dig a deep hole in front of each pillar and find nothing.

After dinner, Uncle Richard called Elizabeth and Jonathan into the sitting room. He opened the glass doors of the high bookcase.

"I found something at the county courthouse." He handed Elizabeth a sheet of paper covered with handwriting. "A photocopy of Peter Rutledge's will."

Elizabeth looked at the paper. The signature on the bottom was large and clear. *Peter F. Rutledge. Peter F.* . . Elizabeth held the paper under a small table lamp. The capital *F* was large and loopy, a little shaky looking.

"Wait! I recognize this handwriting." She bent down closer to the paper. "It's the same as the writing in the old note. Look at this capital *F*. It's just like the *F* in *Friend*."

Uncle Richard hurried over. "But that would mean Peter Rutledge wrote the note about the clue in the teacups."

Elizabeth felt the icy drop of water dripping down her back again. The person leading them to the stolen gift was the thief himself.

Everyone crowded into the small sitting room. Elizabeth set the will on the coffee table next to the old note.

Mr. Pollack sat in an armchair, tapping his chin with his finger. "I hate to be the doubter again, but I do have one problem. Think of the words in the note. *Where it lies hidden I fear to say.* Why would Peter Rutledge write that? What was he afraid of?"

"Maybe he was afraid of admitting to the theft," said Aunt Doris. "Or maybe he had no logical reason. Remember, his mind wasn't right since the war."

Elizabeth pulled her father over to the couch. "Look at the will, Dad. You have to admit, the writing is the same. Especially that capital *F*."

Mr. Pollack took a long look at the papers. "I can't argue with that. You know, I guess detective work is like science. Every time one question is answered, another one pops up. Even after the mystery is solved."

Pop was slumped in a low green armchair. He woke up with a snort that made Aunt Doris's hand fly to her chest.

"Sounds like it's time to turn in," said Uncle Richard. "We'll meet tomorrow morning. Treasure time is at ten o'clock. Diamond Prairie Farm."

Elizabeth didn't sleep well at the E-Z Rest Motor Lodge. The bed springs poked through the thin mattress. Pop snored in the next room like a runaway typhoon. But by morning, that didn't matter. It was a sweet, warm September day. A treasure-hunting day. Elizabeth and Jonathan hurried the grown-ups through breakfast and herded them into the cars well before ten o'clock.

"They're already there. I see their car up ahead." Elizabeth rolled down the window and waved. Aunt Doris and Uncle Richard sat in lawn chairs between the pillars at Diamond Prairie Farm. Behind them, the old white house seemed to slump even farther into the grass.

Uncle Richard stood up. "We're all ready!" A sturdy pickax and two shovels leaned against the stone wall. A picnic cooler sat on a blanket under a tall oak tree. After Aunt Marie helped Pop into a lawn chair, he lit a cigar and stretched out his legs.

"So where do we start digging?" asked Mrs. Pollack. "I mean, in front of which pillar?"

Uncle Richard paced slowly back and forth between the two pillars. He kicked at something with his foot, then bent down and parted the grass. "Question! There's a good-sized rock in the ground in front of this pillar. What would Sherlock Holmes have to say about that?"

"A rock? I don't know, unless . . ." Elizabeth suddenly felt a glimmer of hope. "Unless P. R. put it there to mark the spot where he buried the gift!"

"My thoughts exactly. So this is where we start." Uncle Richard picked up four small stakes and a ball of thin white string. He marked out a three-foot square in front of the pillar. "Let the adventure begin!"

Mr. Pollack hung his jacket on a bush and tied a blue bandanna around his forehead. He brought the pickax down hard, breaking up the thick turf. Pop hoisted himself out of the lawn chair. "Everybody stand back. Stand back, I tell you. That thing could chop off a foot!"

When the dense turf was loosened, the digging began. The heavy black soil didn't give easily. They shoveled two at a time, changing every few minutes. Before long, the hole was a foot deep.

"Watch those shovels!" Pop waved his cigar in the air. "Those things could chop off a foot!"

By eleven o'clock eight jackets were lined up on the stone wall. Aunt Doris passed out cups of lemonade. The buzz of locusts rose and fell in the hot, still air. "Isn't it time for lunch yet?" Jonathan peeked into the cooler and pulled out a cream cheese sandwich on thick homemade bread.

Aunt Marie dropped onto the blanket next to him. "I'm with you, Jon."

As soon as the last sandwich was gone, the digging started again.

"Must be about two feet now. I wonder . . ." Uncle Richard left his sentence dangling. But Elizabeth knew what he was thinking. How long should they keep digging? When should they give up? She half-heartedly took the shovel from Jonathan. Her arms ached, and the shovel seemed to weigh a hundred pounds.

"Oh, great. Another rock." Elizabeth bent over and brushed away the dirt. She could feel something under her hand. Something flat and hard and . . . cold. She fell to her knees and dug with both hands. Mrs. Pollack dropped her shovel with a shout. "Elizabeth found something. Something made of iron!"

Pop rushed over with the others. A dark, rusty lid lay half uncovered at the bottom of the hole. "I've seen plenty of those in my day. That's an old cast iron bean pot."

"A bean pot? But it can't be." Elizabeth brushed the dirt off her knees.

"Here. Let's dig out the whole thing before we open it." Mrs. Pollack quickly dug a circle around the lid. Mr. Pollack helped her pry the rusty pot out of the ground.

"If there's anything in there, at least it will be well protected," said Uncle Richard.

Jonathan watched as the heavy pot was set down on the grass.

"I'll tell you one thing. If that pot is full of moldy old beans, I'm going to give up being a detective. Forever."

Mrs. Pollack turned to Pop. "Why don't you open it, Dad." Pop knelt down and lifted the lid. He reached into the dark opening and pulled out his hand. He was holding something. A small black pouch. Slowly, Pop loosened the cord and tipped the pouch. Elizabeth leaned on her shovel, gripping so tight she couldn't feel her fingers.

Pop pulled away the pouch and held out his hand. Elizabeth reached out but didn't dare touch what she saw. Impossible. Sitting in her grandfather's rough and wrinkled palm was . . . a butterfly. A butterfly with golden wings that glistened with gems. Emeralds. Diamonds. Deep red rubies.

"My word! Those are real jewels!" Aunt Doris fanned herself with her hand. "I've never seen a piece of jewelry like that."

"This pin was meant to be worn on Grandma Lydia's wedding dress," said Uncle Richard. "I'm sure of it."

Elizabeth couldn't take her eyes off the butterfly. It was more beautiful than a thousand chests of pirate's gold. The body was made of three red rubies. The wings were sprinkled with smaller jewels. They sparkled in the light, as if they were shouting for joy at finally seeing the sun.

Jonathan chose a wide oak tree for his Outer Mongolian warrior dance. He grabbed a checkered napkin, trailing it behind him like a flag. Suddenly everyone was talking and laughing.

Pop collapsed into a lawn chair. "I can't believe this! It's like a dream." He looked at Elizabeth and Jonathan. "I guess you two are real detectives now. And darn good ones, at that." He patted his chest. "You take after your old grandpappy. That's for sure."

Elizabeth could only half remember the rest of the day. Back at Elmwood House, a reporter from the local newspaper appeared. He asked questions and wrote down everyone's words in a notebook. Relatives were called; neighbors dropped by. The story of the treasure was told over and over again.

And then, suddenly, it was over. Time to go back to school and work and everyday life. They had one last breakfast together at Elmwood House.

"I can't go, Mom." Elizabeth took her hand off the door of their red car. "I have to look at the butterfly. Just one more time." She ran into the house and slid open the heavy parlor door. The jeweled butterfly sat on a square of black velvet on the old rolltop desk.

"Grandma Lydia would have been proud of you." Uncle Richard walked up from behind. "You and Jonathan finally set things right, just as she wished." He turned toward the window, his brown eyes looking cloudy and soft. "Pop told me you're going to write down some of his stories. I don't know if you'll understand what I'm going to say. But . . . by working on this mystery, you've found more than one treasure."

On Monday morning, Elizabeth hurried to school, bursting to tell her friends about the adventure. She handed her teacher a note, neatly written on plain white stationery. *Please excuse Elizabeth's absence on Friday afternoon. She was digging up buried treasure in Ohio.*

Mrs. Dexter read the note, then sat down at her desk and read it again. "Pay attention, class." She removed her glasses and spoke slowly. "Our Unit Two spelling test for today is canceled. I believe Elizabeth has something to tell us."

At the end of the week Jonathan pulled a large brown envelope out of the mail slot in the front door. "Everybody come downstairs! We got something from Uncle Richard."

The local newspaper was enclosed, with a bold front-page headline:

JUNIOR DETECTIVES SOLVE 120-YEAR-OLD MYSTERY

The article was long and detailed. Even Fritzi was mentioned.

"And here's some good news from Uncle Richard." Mrs. Pollack held a typewritten letter in her hand. "Mr. Applegate isn't interested in the Diamond Prairie Farm anymore. You see, he thought a big four-lane highway was going to be built out that way. But now it looks like the highway won't be built. So all his big plans have come to nothing."

"Well, I'm glad," said Elizabeth. "But what about the butterfly? Who gets to keep it?"

Mrs. Pollack turned over the letter. "Let's see. Uncle Richard says that he and Pop talked to their cousins about it. They decided Pop should have the jewels, since he's the oldest in the family. There's one condition though." She folded up the letter. "The butterfly is never to be sold. It's going to be handed down in the family from generation to generation. That way the treasure will never be lost again."

Mr. Pollack stood between Jonathan and Elizabeth and put his arms around their shoulders. "Well, if you ask me, I'd say this mystery has come to a perfect end."

End? Elizabeth didn't like the word *end*. It made her feel sad and restless, like reading the very last words of a good book. She crossed her arms and took a good look at Jonathan. His thick, brown hair was a fright, as usual. He had jelly stains on his T-shirt and a rubber salamander hanging out of his pocket. But then again, he *could* be a good detective. With some expert training.

Elizabeth took her lucky green pen out of her pocket and gave it a click. "Do you know what, Dad? I have a strange feeling that this is just the beginning."

Become a memory keeper in your family

Here are some ideas to get you started:

♦ Put together a memory box. Help your parents or grandparents collect some interesting items from their past. Make sure the items are labelled and explained, if necessary. Many different things can be put in a memory box—old letters, postcards, reports cards, newspaper clippings, wedding invitations, medals. Perhaps part of a wedding dress, a piece of jewelry, or some old buttons or toys could be included. For the box itself, you could decorate a shoe box, or you could use a round hat box or an old-fashioned suitcase.

♦ Start your own memory box. Choose some small objects—things you might want to look back on when you're older. And don't forget to describe some of the games you play. Write down your favorite clapping rhymes or jump rope rhymes, or describe an outside game you like to play. The box itself can be part of the memory. How about your favorite old lunch box or a box one of your toys came in?

♦ Do your parents or other family members remember any family stories, fairy tales, or folk tales told to them as children? Write down your favorites or make a tape recording.

◆   Is there an old box of family things in the attic or in the back of a closet? Go through it with a relative and find out what's in there. Who knows? You might find a mystery or a puzzle to be solved.

◆   Be a director! Make a video or tape recording of older family members talking about their past. They may remember things you read about in history books. Don't forget the funny things and the everyday things. What was their school day like? Did they ever play a good joke on someone? Make a list of questions to help them get started.

◆   Start a collection of favorite recipes from family or friends. Learn how to make them by helping or watching. Note down any story connected with the recipe.

◆   Find an object with a story to tell. Is there something in your house or in a relative's house that holds a special memory? Perhaps something was brought here from another country or was a special gift or has been handed down in the family. Write down the story and draw a picture to go with it.

◆   At your next holiday celebration, get a few people to tell about their most memorable holiday. Warn them ahead of time so they have time to think about it. Write down or tape your favorite story. Make sure to get the facts right, just like a newspaper reporter!

◆   Ask your parents and grandparents to write down names and birth dates of family members for as many generations as they can. You'll have the beginnings of a family tree. Were some people on your family tree born in another country? See if you can find their birthplaces on a map.

◆   Look in the library under *genealogy*. There are good books which will give you more ideas. The books will explain how to make a family tree and how to look through records to solve some of the puzzles you will encounter when you start delving into family history. The Internet, of 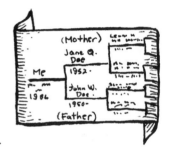 course, has many sites on genealogy. Under *genealogy, genealogy for beginners*, or *hobbies and interests: genealogy*, you can find lists of web sites, reviews of software, newsletters, books, and much more. Some search engines will list the top-rated web sites.